RELENTLESS

JADE WEST

CHAPTER ONE

Elaine

F OR ALL THE weirdness in my life, nothing felt weirder than waking up in bed next to the man I'd grown up believing to be my worst enemy. Weirder still was being madly in love with him. The world was upside down. I was consumed by the devotion I felt for Lucian Morelli.

It felt even more bizarre for the fact there was a body buried in the backyard…and I felt happy about that. Relieved about that. Loving life with a passion I thought I'd never feel.

The Morelli monster had killed the monster who'd abused me.

He killed Reverend Lynch. For me.

It was early morning. The light was barely showing outside. I snuggled closer to Lucian and took a breath, enjoying the steadiness of his.

He was a deep sleeper. Beautiful.

I don't know how long I lay there at his side before he moved and turned toward me. It felt like hours of perfect bliss, but in reality it was barely more than minutes. The light was shining brighter outside, but not by much. The day was still only just beginning.

Lucian's arms were around me before he woke, holding me with the kind of strength that made my heart sing. He was possessive, even in a dream state.

His eyes focused on mine just as soon as he opened them.

Neither of us moved. Our faces were barely inches apart, breaths matching.

His heat was divine.

It was his cell phone that broke the spell. He fumbled a strong hand to the nightstand and looked at the screen. "It's my cousin. Elliot Morelli."

The word was a slap, even as I sat there, even as he took the call.

I thought of him as Lucian. I thought of him as a monster. I didn't mind that he was a Morelli, not anymore, but the world would mind. The sound of the other person on the phone was tinny and indistinct. I couldn't make it out, but I could feel the way Lucian tensed. He pushed up to sit down, revealing a strong, muscled back and the barest hint of his ass. He was unselfconscious, which made sense, because he was perfect. Sculpted by Michelangelo. I couldn't enjoy the view, because tension spread like a virus.

He gave a couple terse responses, but I still didn't know what was happening.

I only knew that it was bad.

He hung up with a muttered curse word.

"What's wrong?" I asked, almost afraid to hear the answer. But he'd heard it. He'd heard it with a stoic courage that I wanted to match.

"Someone put out a hit."

A hit. It took me a long second to understand what he meant. Not a hit of cocaine. Not a hit like a punch to the face. He meant a hit like murder. "On me?"

"On both of us."

I gasped. "Why?"

"You know why. It was okay when we were fucking. But now that we care about each other, they're worried. And they want it to stop."

I sat up with him, struggling to make sense of things. A few minutes ago I'd been luxuriating in a love-drenched haze. Now my heart beats a million miles a second. I knew we were forbidden, of course. Star-crossed lovers, our families at war.

But I thought that meant fights over the dinner table. I thought that meant being ostracized or cut off. I thought that meant angry actions taken through business leverage. I didn't know it meant assassination. "Who?" I manage.

"I don't know, and I'm not sure it even matters. My father, probably. Though it could be your mother using her resident fixer Ronan Byrne. And that's to say nothing of the Power Brothers."

He was right. It wouldn't make any difference who'd given the order when we were dead. Nothing could stop the truth. We were in danger with every passing second.

Out there in the big savage world beyond Bishop's Landing, and the diamond of a house we shared, our families were part of one hell of a war.

Constantines vs Morellis, just like always.

Only now the Power Brothers were up against the Constantines too.

Blamed for my disappearance and kidnapping.

Yeah, it would be getting seriously damn bad out there, and if anyone should find out that it wasn't the Power Brothers who had taken me from my NYC apartment...that it was Lucian Morelli I was with... "It can't be my mother. She doesn't know it's you."

"Then it's only a matter of time until she wants my blood, too. They'll find out it was me, eventually. Maybe all of them will put out hits on us. They'll kill us again and again until there's nothing left. No children to betray the family pride."

My thoughts were in chaos.

I had nothing to say, so I didn't say a word, I just kissed him.

That was the only answer I had to give.

I kissed the beautiful monster, and he kissed me back. Hard. Really damn hard. Love and lust are a heady combination, an ocean more welcome than thoughts of our doom.

His hands pinned mine above my head and he ravaged me, flesh to flesh. My legs parted and wrapped around his waist and his movements were raw. Fierce.

I was still sore from where he'd taken me the night before. He'd played me like an instrument into the early hours of the morning, teasing, tempting, hurting. Loving me.

I was more than ready for him when his cock pushed inside me on a fresh new day. My moans were as raw as his thrusts, my hips pushing back up to meet his.

We were still in the rhythm when his cell rang again. He ignored it. It sounded out again. He ignored it, but I felt him flinch. I knew he was hearing the danger as loud as I was.

He hit the spot just right inside me when it sounded out again and I was coming for him, just as they were out there coming for us. I was squirming under him while he slammed, slammed, slammed, but it was more than the *want*. It was the fear that had my pulse racing along with my desperation for the man I loved.

He came at the height of my crescendo, breaths ragged when he let his weight crush down onto mine. His cell sounded out again and we were both feeling it. Both scared.

It terrified me even more to sense Lucian's fear than it ever would to feel my own.

"Are you going to get that call?" I asked him.

"I'm going to have to very soon." He rolled off me with a sigh and took my hand. "That was a lovely distraction but we really are fucked, you know. Maybe your family and the Power Brothers will wipe each other out and we won't have to worry."

"Maybe," I said, but my voice was weak.

His eyes spoke more than words. Heavy. "We both know that's not going to happen," he told me. "We're in serious fucking danger."

The thought stabbed me in the stomach.

The idea of the carnage happening in the world outside was a hard one to take. Families at war, over me, over us. People thinking they were lashing out to rescue me from kidnapping or death—if they didn't believe I was dead and gone already.

The warfare outside was because of me.

I let out a sigh. "Maybe they won't actually find out it was you. Maybe we can stay holed up here forever and nobody will ever think to look in Bishop's Landing. Maybe this can be the Lucian and Elaine paradise, immune from the world."

"I love your stunning optimism. I wish it had a scrap of a chance of being true."

The Morelli god got out of bed and slipped on some sweatpants as I watched him. I'd never seen him so casual and it suited him. His body really was a masterpiece, sculpted to perfection. His pants sat down low on his hips, the V of him proud.

There was no protest from him today as I dipped straight into his closet and pulled out one of his shirts. I slipped it on over my head as he watched me right back.

"You really are a beautiful creature," he said,

and it made me glow.

I could have flicked on the TV on our way through to the kitchen. But I couldn't face the barrage of news about my abduction. I couldn't face seeing my sisters crying, begging people to contact the authorities with any news of my disappearance. I didn't want to see the specula-tion, and the stories, and the hotlines for reporting information. I had too many feelings swirled together—guilt, fear, and irrepressible love.

Lucian had his phone with him but he wasn't looking at it. That's when I got a sense of it again—that simmering tension under his skin, knowing even better than I did just how the world would be coming for us.

We headed right through to the kitchen for coffee, neither of us acknowledging the calls he was trying his best to ignore.

I shot a glance out of the window, and my mind was right back on the body buried out there under the flower beds.

"What you did to Reverend Lynch, Lucian…I don't even know how to say thanks for that. Is it even right that I'm happy he's dead? Does that make me a bad person?"

"Of course you're happy he's dead," he told

me, deadpan. "If I could have prolonged his suffering any more, I'd have done it. As it is, the ground is soaked in his blood."

I knew I was blushing. "Thank you."

"You're welcome," he said, and he meant it. I could see it in his eyes.

I chose to face up to the obvious. "How long do you think we'll be able to stay here?" I asked him, and he shrugged.

"Days, tops. Questions will start needing answers. Bullets will start flying. Every scrap of the war will lead them closer to the core."

Even the thought of it had my stomach twisting. "Then we run?"

"You would really do that?" he asked. "You would run away from everything you've ever known?"

My nod was frantic. "I'd run right now. Together."

He was quiet, pondering. Staring out through the window as I stared at him. "I haven't a damn clue where we would go. Our families have reach in every place we could run to. They'd be after us, chasing us down every single day for the rest of our lives."

I couldn't hold back my flood of emotion. "And every single day would be worth it."

He leaned against the counter. "You might not be saying that when we're running around the globe like a couple of escaped convicts, living from a suitcase."

"What's the alternative?" I asked. "Waiting here until they find out you were the one who took me and hunt us down? We could always try the double suicide option."

"The alternative is that you head back into the city," he said. "You tell them the Power Brothers did this, or some random criminal on the street, or whatever the hell you want to tell them, and go back home. Regardless of how pissed your mother is, she won't let you stay on the streets. She won't let you die. You'd be back home safely."

My reply was instant. Strong and fierce. "*This* is home. With you."

The stare between us was intense. My heart thumped, hard. I meant it.

This was home. *He* was home.

His thumb brushed my cheek as he stepped up close, and my body was alive with the scent of him, the touch of him, the heat of him. "I'm glad to hear it," he said. "Just remember that I gave you the option once you have a gun barrel in your face, saying your holy goodbyes."

"That wouldn't matter," I whispered. "Saying

my holy goodbyes, I'd still be happy that I'd spent the last of them with you. With you inside me. Loving me."

That's when the beautiful monster surprised me more than ever. "It's not just your body I want to be inside. I want to be inside your mind, your hopes, your fears. Your quirks and your laughter. Your whole fucking soul."

It slammed me, right in my heart. I felt like a little girl again, praying that I'd be good enough for someone to love me one day.

We were kissing when his cell started up again.

"Jesus fucking Christ," he cursed, finally pulling away far enough to take hold of the phone. "It's the devil himself. Bryant Morelli. Well, he was always a brazen son of a bitch."

Chapter Two

Lucian

NOT IN THE slightest. The days were counting down to hours, to minutes. All of them leading to our doom. Was Bryant Morelli calling to gloat?

"Good morning," I said, knowing full well that it would be anything but good.

"What have you done? What have you fucking done?"

This shock seemed genuine, but then again he was a smart man. A manipulative man. Right now he seemed the most likely source of the kill order. "You knew I was going after Elaine. You knew I picked her over the company."

"You're a traitor," he growled. "And you're an idiot to match. You must have been trying to get yourself killed, fucking around with a Constantine. They aren't going to stand for it."

"Are you going to stand for it?" I asked softly.

"Come home. We need to strategize. We need to make a plan."

"I'm busy."

"Your mother is crying her eyes out."

"How do I know I'm not going to get shot as soon as I walk into the door?"

There's a pause. "Are you fucking kidding me?"

"No."

"Are you suggesting that I put out a hit on my own son?"

"Spare me the outrage. Someone did. And you aren't exactly the picture of fatherly love. I tried to take over Morelli Holdings. That was before I committed the ultimate sin—caring about a Constantine."

"We all make mistakes," he says, his voice wry.

The way he said it made me wonder if he'd made similar mistakes. I knew the takeover of Morelli Holdings from his father hadn't been a peaceful one. I wouldn't have expected any less from my father. It was practically a family tradition for the Morellis.

It made me wonder if he'd made similar mistakes about forbidden women. It would explain why he hated the Constantines so much. And why he'd refused to really take action against them now that Caroline was a widow. Did he secretly want her?

None of that mattered.

I would have a better sense of my father's intentions in person. And if it was him, then the hit was more than a simple desire to have me dead. It was a power play. And the way to react to a power play wasn't to fucking run. It was to face him.

"I'm on my way," I said and I ended the call.

"What is it?" Elaine asked, and her beautiful eyes were wide open.

Even in that moment of horror I couldn't stop the flood of adoration I felt for the stunning creature before me.

Her blonde curls were messy in the most gorgeous of ways, framing her perfect face like a halo. She was a goddess. The most divine little doll in creation.

I've never been a man to share anything with anyone. I never talked about any of my business, any of my personal associations, any of my actions, but with her it flowed naturally.

"That was my father. I'm going to see him."

Her eyes widened. "Won't that make you a

target?"

"Yes," I said honestly. "I'll be careful, but I want you to lock the front door when I've gone. If I'm not back by dusk, I want you to head to the Constantine Compound."

Her mouth dropped open, scared. "Then don't go," she whispered. "Please, Lucian, just don't go. We could run now. We could run…"

I took her hands in mine. "We wouldn't get very far, sweetheart. Not like this. We don't have the network in place to get out of here without getting caught. If people are talking about us. If people know *anything* about us, then we are absolutely fucked."

"Please…" she started, but I squeezed her fingers.

"We pray, Elaine. We pray that I can change our fates. That's the only reason I'm going in right now. The only reason I'd leave you alone for even a minute."

She didn't argue because there would be no point and she knew it.

My mind was already set.

I headed upstairs and took a shower. There was nothing but a few minutes of hot steam to set me up for the day before I toweled myself down and got myself suited up and ready.

She waited anxiously at the bottom of the stairs when I came down. "Are you sure this is okay? What if he attacks you?"

"Unlikely," I told her. "He knows I would fight back. If he's going to kill me, more likely he'll do it through someone he pays. I'll do everything I can to divert the smoke from the fire, but the fire is there, Elaine, and it's burning bright."

She wrapped her arms around me like a blanket before I walked out of the front door, pressing so tight to me that I could feel her thumping heart. "Be safe."

"I'm serious," I whispered, right in her ear. "If I'm not here by dusk, you head to the Constantine Compound. You stay the fuck alive. Promise."

"Okay," she said, but I knew she was lying. I could hear it in her voice.

I pulled away enough to take hold of her jaw. "You swear to me, Elaine. If I'm not back here by dusk, you head home. You let your mother protect you."

She stalled. I could see the lie dancing behind her eyes.

"This is one thing we get straight, right from the beginning," I told her. "You don't lie to me.

However bad the truth is, you never lie to me, sweetheart. Is that understood?"

The lie disappeared. I saw it loud and clear in that moment. Elaine Constantine wouldn't lie to me, not once she'd sworn her loyalty. "I won't lie to you," she said. "I swear it."

"Good girl," I said and kissed her forehead.

Handing over the keys to her felt surreal. Handing control of anything to another person felt surreal.

I said it once more to be sure. "If I'm not back here by dusk—"

She was nodding when she interjected. "I'll stay alive. I swear it."

I said something I thought I'd never say. It rolled off my tongue like the easiest words I'd ever spoken. "I love you."

Her smile was perfection. "I love you, too."

I kissed her once, hard, and then I walked away.

The drive to my parents' house was short.

The butler nodded his head when I entered. *Good morning, Mr. Morelli, sir.*

I tipped my head at them, keeping my expression as stoic as ever.

My father would be in his study floor nine. I knew he'd be at the very end of the management suite meeting rooms, awaiting me with his evil eyes and his pitted jaw.

I wasn't mistaken.

"Sit the fuck down," he said, and I did as instructed, sitting back in my seat with my foot up on one knee.

"What is this about?" I asked him, my voice barely more than a hiss to match.

He tossed a file across at me and I flicked it open.

Testimonials of clubgoers saying how they'd seen Lucian Morelli chasing down Elaine Constantine. The event where I'd floored the security guard after the pathetic little downtown dive was recorded loud and clear.

"How do you think this fucking looks?" he said. "I knew you'd been chasing that Constantine, but I didn't expect the whole fucking world to be talking about it. The Constantines are entering a discussion with the Power Brothers. A fucking *discussion.* It should be bloodshed, not conversation, and this is because of you, isn't it? We were set to pair up with the Powers, not watch from the sidelines as they begin negotiations."

My blood chilled even colder than its usual ice. Discussions were never good, not between enemies. They showed nothing more than that people were prepared to hear alternate versions of events.

"Tell me now," my father said. "Is there anything I should know about this?"

I looked him right in the eyes. "Such as what?"

"Such as you chasing down Elaine Constantine. Did you kill her?"

My answer was perfectly truthful. "No. I didn't kill her."

"So the Powers have her, yes? Their negotiations with the Constantines will be futile?"

"What the Powers have and don't have has never been high on my list of priorities. I can sure as hell not answer questions for them." Again, I wasn't lying.

My father's glare was savage. "If the Constantines and the Power Brothers come to some crazy conclusion that we're responsible for this, Lucian, life sure as fuck isn't going to be easy."

He was right on that front. The Constantines we could take on, happily. It would be a difficult battle, but it would be a fair one. For us to go up against the Constantines with the Power Brothers also on their side would be a whole other matter.

"We could have paired up with the Powers,"

he said. "You know full well they wanted our allegiance. We could have made a powerful ally."

"Yes," I replied. "I know that. Maybe they still will."

"Then it should be *us* they are entering into discussions with, not the fucking Constantines." He gestured to the file in front of me. "Tell me about this. What do I need to know about your relentless pursuit of that little blonde?"

I shrugged at him. "I was chasing her. It got intense."

His stare was ruthless. "I'll get to the bottom of this, boy, and you know it. If there is anything you need to tell me, you'd better do it now."

"I have nothing to say." In that very moment I was sealing my demise.

"Get out of here, then," he said. "Get your head straight with whatever pussy you want to indulge in and then get the fuck back to work."

"Fine," I said, and got to my feet. "I'll enjoy my fucking *vacation*."

He called me back when I got to the door.

"I mean it, Lucian," he said. "If you've done anything to jeopardize our family name or position in this world, I'll kill you myself. People are talking, and they're talking now. If you think for a second you are one step ahead of anyone, you are very sorely mistaken. They're coming for you, and I will be too if you've let me down. Believe me."

I had no doubt about that as I turned my back on him and walked away.

CHAPTER THREE

Elaine

I WAS PETRIFIED, wandering through the house like a ghost, praying, praying, praying that my love would come back to me before dusk. The front door was locked, just like I promised it would be. I couldn't stop looking at it. Pacing back and forth, back and forth, back and forth.

Up and down the hallway like a woman possessed.

My mind was churning through the maybes.

Maybe people had found out about where I was. Maybe they'd found out that my note blaming the Power Brothers was just more of my lies. Maybe this whole new beautiful part of my world would last just a few tiny days before fate laughed in my face and gave me the middle finger.

I'd sworn to Lucian that I'd head back into the city if he didn't come home. Heading back into the city would be the last thing I'd ever want to do again. Not ever.

It turns out fate wasn't such a vindictive beast after all. Thank the Lord.

My heart was a racing train when I heard the car pull up into the driveway. My fingers were shaking as I twisted the key in the lock to let him in. I almost swung the door off its hinges as I burst my way out there to meet him.

My exclamation was loud. "Lucian!"

His arms answered me when he stepped up onto the porch. They wrapped me up so tightly it was heaven, squeezing me safe.

I pulled away enough to stare up at him, my eyes searching his face.

His expression was solid, like steel, but there was something in his gaze. Something that told me fate hadn't been quite so kind after all.

He didn't launch straight into an explanation.

"What was it?" I asked him. "Was it work?"

"No, sweetheart. It wasn't work."

We went through to the kitchen and he propped himself against the counter, but his stare was anything but relaxed. "The Power Brothers are entering into discussions with your family."

I'm sure my mouth must have dropped open. "Discussions? But what the hell have they got to be talking about? My family thinks the Power Brothers killed me to clear my debts…"

"This is the problem," he said. "Apparently they aren't quite so sure that is the case anymore. It appears the Power Brothers are intent on making that clear, and everyone else is likely believing them."

I felt a flood of panic in me, because if my family didn't believe my note was telling the truth…If they started asking questions which led them closer to reality…

Lucian made us coffees that neither of us had an interest in.

"My father had a file full of witness statements. People telling tales about how I was chasing you through clubs downtown. Even the security guard I kneed in the gut was fool enough to tell the world it was me who did that to him. Under usual circumstances he'd pay for that. I'd have him torn to pieces."

"Does he believe them, your father?" I asked. "Does he think it was you who took me?"

He sipped his coffee. "He asked me if I killed you. I said no."

I let out a breath. "Maybe they won't find out what really happened. Who knows? Maybe my family will attack the Power Brothers before they ever realize they didn't get to me in time. Because they would have taken me, the Power Brothers...I really did see them hunting me down. They would have killed me."

He shook his head. "Your friend Tristan hasn't spoken up yet. That singer he was hooked up with hasn't either, but if they do. *When* they do." He paused. "Or when they realize that Reverend Lynch has been taken from the manor. So many things, baby. It's only a matter of time."

My soul was shriveling, because he was right. The roads all led to Lucian. To me and Lucian. Even my cousin Silas had seen us together, back at Tinsley's birthday ball. As soon as the Power Brothers were out of the equation, it would be like an atom bomb, waiting right at our door, ready to explode.

"So what do we do?" I asked him. "We have to do something, right? There has to be something we can do, because I can't go back there. I can't, Lucian."

"Every second is one step closer to our doom," he told me. "We have to move. Quickly."

I was nodding, frantic. "Yes, we move! We move anywhere! I don't care where we go, just as long as I'm with you. Please, Lucian, let's run. Let's run now!"

His cell sounded out again. A message. He picked it up and I watched his face as he read it. I saw his mouth drop. "That's my cousin, Elliot Morelli. He's asking me what the hell is going on. Says everyone is talking about Lucian Morelli and Elaine Constantine and how I've been hunting you down."

My head was spinning, trying to work out some miracle solution. I'd been a fool to think a single note would condemn the Power Brothers for wiping me out without anyone questioning a thing. Only I hadn't cared about Lucian Morelli then. Not enough to attempt something less questionable.

Lucian's fingers were still hitting his cell screen.

"I'll make some calls," he said. "Get an exit plan together."

"An exit plan?"

"Fake IDs. We need to get out of here, overseas as soon as possible."

"Okay. Right," I said. "I guess you have loads of them, right? Fake IDs and stuff. I know people do. People like you, I mean."

He sneered, but there was affection in it. "*People like me.* I love how you've been raised to believe that I really am some monster from the underworld and your family is on the other end of the spectrum. Believe me, sweetheart, your family will have as many fake IDs as mine will. They're as fucked up in the evil shit as we are."

I tipped my head. "Yeah, okay, well, *I* don't have any fake IDs. I've never seen one in my life."

He smirked. "I love your innocence."

I rolled my eyes. "Not many people would say a party girl with a debt so huge that it would cost her her life had a huge amount of innocence about her."

"Still," he said. "You're innocent. I love you for it."

Hearing those words from him made my soul sing. *I love you.* Lucian Morelli really loved me. A Morelli really did love a Constantine.

And a Constantine loved him right back.

"You know this is like some fucked-up version of Romeo and Juliet, right?" I said. "It's like a modern-day Shakespeare, just a whole load less…picturesque."

I adored his smile, even though it was a sad one. "Just a shame Romeo and Juliet both die at the end of it, isn't it? Let's do our best to make sure we don't follow in their fucking footsteps."

He finished his coffee and wandered away with his cell in his hand, fingers busy. I finished mine and headed through to the living room, daring to put the TV on to check out the latest news.

It was all still the same, pleas for information from my family and people saying random shit about where they'd seen me. It seemed the mainstream media wasn't anywhere closer to the truth. I doubted they ever would be.

I could hear Lucian speaking, his voice low and his tone his usual icy pitch. I didn't focus on what he was saying. There was a strange calmness in me somehow, even with the looming carnage. It was trust. I trusted Lucian to take care. Of me. Of us.

He was gone a while before he came through to the living room.

"The UK," he said to me. "We'll go abroad. We'll be running, but we stand more chance of surviving with the Atlantic Ocean as a buffer, at least."

I hadn't been overseas since I was a little girl. We'd gone there as a family, smiling for the cameras as we checked out London with a few of the aristocrats we were such good family friends with. I'd been in awe of the place. I'd loved it. The London Eye and Buckingham Palace and the quaint countryside surrounding the city.

"Can we get there?" I asked him. "Will we manage to make the journey?"

"Only one way to find out."

One thing was for sure, I'd risk my life trying.

Chapter Four

Lucian

We were fighting time and I knew it. The tentacles were snaking closer to us. Questions hissing closer and closer.

I'd managed to find out that the Constantines were meeting the Power Brothers at that very moment. We had hours, tops, before those discussions would lead to our demise, or get very close to it. As soon as the Constantines stopped looking at the Power Brothers and shot even the slightest glance in another direction, we'd be fucked, and my father had his pulse in line with theirs, seeking out my lies.

The contacts I chose to use were distant from my regular network—as distant as I could possibly risk venturing. I mentioned nothing about Elaine Constantine being alongside me, just that I needed a fresh set of IDs to get out of the country.

Wesley Dale was all set to meet me in the parking lot of JFK International Airport, but it would be over twenty-four hours until he could deliver. As well as the fake IDs, he was also getting us tickets on a flight out of there.

As much as twenty-four hours between now and our flight would be one hell of a long one, it did grant me a window to complete the calling in my soulless heart that couldn't be silenced.

I had something that needed to be done first, before we made our escape. Something I couldn't walk away from. Something I could never leave the country without fulfilling, no matter how insane it might be. It was festering too deep in my gut to ignore.

There was no guarantee I'd ever be back in the US again in this lifetime. This might well be my one and only chance to deliver what was deserved to the pieces of filth.

I'd do my damn fucking best trying.

I gave Elaine one more chance to back out of a future on the run before we were snared for good.

"You're really sure about this? This is your last opportunity to head back to your world. Make sure you won't regret the road you take with me, sweetheart."

Her reply was instant. "I'd rather die with you than survive alone."

It was a beautiful statement. One I fully reciprocated as I pulled her close and held her tight.

"Ditto."

Her smile was amazing.

"Let's go, then, Romeo. Let's get across the ocean and start our new life."

That's when I told her, my eyes fixed firm on hers.

"Our escape will be tomorrow, which is just as well. I have something I need to do before then, Juliet."

Her question was instant. Wide-eyed.

"What? What do you need to do before then?"

I contemplated sharing my plans, but I didn't. She would only beg me to let them go, but I had no intention of it. I wouldn't let retribution go for any fucking thing in the world.

It wasn't only fake IDs and plane tickets and women's clothes I'd been seeking out on my cell for the past sixty minutes. It was Colonel Hardwick's current location. Only that had led me to so much more. You could call it God giving me his blessing. I fucking deserved it for the beautiful payback I was about to deliver.

Through my backhanded investigations, I'd managed to find out that it wasn't just Colonel Hardwick who was at Hanborough Park Golf Course that morning. No. Lionel Constantine, the depraved uncle who'd delivered Elaine to her abusers when she was just a scared little girl, was right there with him. A forty minute drive away.

Halle-fucking-lujah.

I knew what they were there for. I knew the only thing they could possibly be there socializing for in the midst of Elaine Constantine's abduction. Reverend Lynch. The vile priest and his sudden disappearance, and no doubt the girls I'd set free to run away from the manor late that night after I'd taken his sicko life away from him.

I changed my clothes to casual golfing attire as Elaine stared on from the bedroom doorway. She was visibly scared as I loaded myself up with the necessary weaponry from the cabinet downstairs. She was ghostly as she followed me around the place, eyes wide and terrified.

"Really, Lucian, whatever it is you *need* to do, do you really have to do it? We could hole up here and stay as quiet as we can, and just pray that nobody finds us."

I stepped up close and took hold of her chin, tipping her face up to mine.

"I need to go. I can't leave without delivering what's due."

She was shaking as I kissed her. She let out a breath as my tongue pushed its way inside her mouth and danced with a passion. Kissing stopped her questions.

"There are suitcases under the bed in my room," I told her as I forced myself to pull away. "If you want to make our escape as smooth as possible, then please feel free to pack as many essentials as you can find for the journey. The more ready we are to leave, the better. Somehow we need to find you some damn clothes to go with, too. I don't think you wearing my shirt on the plane is going to blend us into the hustle all that much."

She smiled at me and did a scared little curtsy. "I kinda like wearing your shirt constantly. Can't say I've been missing my wardrobe."

I did my best to smile right back at her. "Lock the door behind me again. Same rules apply. I'm not back by dusk, you head back to the city."

This time her nod was quiet, her meekness visible. The sassy doll who'd fired back at me at every opportunity just a few days earlier was well out of sight.

Surprisingly, I was looking forward to her

return.

I was off quickly, slipping into the car and driving away with a screech of tires as she watched from the doorstep, arms wrapped around her chest.

I called up the navigation on my cell and sped toward my destination. I had my own membership to Hanborough Park, nobody would question my arrival.

There wasn't even the faintest sliver of uncertainty in me as I pulled up into the golf course parking lot. I was as sure of my actions as I'd been of anything in my life. My fingers were already itching to pull the trigger and deliver revenge on behalf of the woman I loved.

"Good morning," I said to the guy at the check-in desk when I stepped into reception.

"Good morning, Mr. Morelli, sir," he offered and waved me on through. He was new to the position. I'd never seen him before.

New enough not to know that you keep Morellis and Constantines apart at all costs.

I used that to my advantage.

"I'm here to meet up with Colonel Hardwick. Could you please tell me which hole he's on?"

He gave me a happy little smile. "Last time I heard they were at hole four, but I'm not sure."

I would have to take his advice and hope for the best. Hole four was very isolated. There wouldn't be a passerby for quite some time—at least I hoped not.

"Thank you," I said to the fool who'd shared their privacy, and then I walked on through.

I knew where I was headed. My pace was quick and determined, ensuring I stayed on the edges of the course and out of view of the stragglers of golfers in the distance. Every single moment I could delay people identifying me as the culprit behind this attack was a tick for our odds of managing to reach the UK.

I couldn't take a golf cart, but I'd been walking no more than ten minutes when the two pieces of shit appeared on the horizon. I slowed down my pace, being more sure than ever to keep hidden as I approached. They were talking heatedly. I could see the waving of their arms, golf clearly the last thing on their minds.

I knew then, beyond all doubt, that they were aware Reverend Lynch had encountered some...*difficulties.*

I kept to the rough as I walked, heart thumping and blood ice cold and burning bright with the promise of vengeance. My gun was aching to fire and my fingers were aching to set the bullets free, right into the guts of them.

I slipped on my leather gloves and was already holding the gun when I appeared in view. They were talking so intently that they didn't notice me until I was close enough that they could hear me clear my throat.

Both sick fucks jumped a mile when they saw me there, starting backwards once they registered it was me.

Hardwick stepped away from Lionel Constantine, clearly happy to abandon him for his demise. So much for friendship and loyalty. He was clearly ready to run, his hands held up in front of him as I stepped up closer.

"This is between you two," he told me. "I'll leave you to your family dispute and head on to the next hole."

"Get the hell fucking back here," I snarled at him. "This has plenty to do with the both of you, you disgusting piece of shit."

I watched his mind whirring. I smirked as I saw the pieces come together for him, while Lionel Constantine was still staring on in mute horror.

"You're attacking the fellowship, yes?" Hardwick announced, his wavering voice scared enough to set my heart alight. "The fellowship has nothing against the Morellis, I can assure you of that."

"This isn't about the fucking Morellis," I told him with a vicious smile. "This is to do with Elaine."

"Elaine?!" Hardwick gasped. "You mean Elaine Constantine?"

That's when Lionel found his voice. "You just *killed* Elaine Constantine," he said, and there wasn't even the slightest hint of anger in his voice. "What the fuck has that got to do with coming after the fellowship?"

I laughed to myself at their ridiculous attempt at feigning ignorance.

"You know exactly what coming after the fellowship has to do with Elaine Constantine," I told them. "You fucking *abused* Elaine Constantine when she was a pure little girl, you sick cunts."

I pointed the gun at them, the silencer already in place. Their shock was evident, but not nearly so evident as their fear. They were absolutely petrified. Their own doom looming loud and clear.

"What the hell are you doing?" Lionel said. "Like you give a fuck about Elaine."

"I love your beautiful angel of a niece," I told

him. "Just be grateful I don't have longer to make you suffer even more for your crimes."

His eyes were open right on mine when I pulled the trigger. One lonely bullet, right in his face.

He was gone. Hardwick started stumbling, trying to run. The sad, bloated prick didn't get very far before I was up and at him, tearing him backwards and spinning him to face the corpse I'd just landed into hell.

"No!" he cried out as I forced the gun in his hand and grasped his fingers around it. He fought, but I was stronger. His hand was clutching the gun when I turned it around and pressed the barrel up against his temple.

"*Please,*" he begged me, squirming like a slug in my arms. "Please, no!"

"Good night, motherfucker," I said, and then I shot him.

Only *I* didn't shoot him, did I? It was *his* finger on the trigger.

The sad, miserable fucker had shot himself. Appeared to the onlooker that he'd shot Lionel Constantine before blowing himself away, too.

Oh, the bliss of inflicting that much hurt. I was back in my school days again, enjoying the suffering. Only this was better. More fulfilling than ever. Delivering Elaine's revenge was the most rewarding torture I'd ever given.

I was running out of time with the shots ringing out, and I knew it. The course was big and people were distant, but they were audible. Questions would surely be asked, and asked quickly.

I got the fuck out of there as quickly as I fucking could.

Only it wasn't quick enough. Not as the dominos started tumbling.

My cell was alive with news and whispers. My father as close to the tendrils as anyone else on the scene. They were coming for us. Right fucking now.

CHAPTER FIVE

Elaine

I STARTED PACKING as soon as the car had left the driveway. My hands were jittery, but that was okay. It was good to have them occupied.

It took barely any time before I'd folded and packed almost every item of clothing from Lucian's closet. I'd boxed up several pairs of his shoes, and the bulk of toiletries we wouldn't need to use before leaving, and then I'd dug into his most private space and packed his dream journal and fountain pen and the watch with RHM on the leather strap. I was on a mission, getting us ready to roll.

My jitters were even worse when I was done. I drifted aimlessly around the place, chewing at my nails, staying inside with the door locked—just like I promised Lucian. As much as the grass outside was calling me, tempting me to head outside for some fresh air, I wouldn't break my promise. As much as I wanted to venture out and see the mound of dirt we'd thrown over Reverend Lynch's body, I didn't. I didn't break my promise to Lucian.

Still, I'd stare at it from the window. I'd stare at that dirty grave and think of the disgusting body inside it with a flame down deep inside me. *Fuck you, you sick asshole.*

I was so fucking glad he was dead.

Reverend Lynch's pit of a resting place was a beacon, thrilling me, but there was more to it than that. I couldn't deny the thoughts that were tickling my mind. Thoughts of what Lucian might be doing as I waited for him to come home that could be so damn important. So damn important, and so private that he had chosen to keep it from me.

Where could he be?

If he wasn't at Morelli Holdings, and we weren't getting flights on our escape run until tomorrow, then where the hell could Lucian be?

I knew there was something dark and deep about what he'd headed off to do, stepping out into the world when we should surely be hiding in here as quietly as we could and counting down the minutes. I also knew, just an inkling, but a powerful one, that what he was doing had something to do with *me*. I was still in shock about that—a powerful beast of a man like Lucian on a mission to do something for a little fuckup of a girl like *me*.

There was a strange pleasure to it, better than the greatest cocaine buzz I'd ever felt. It made my heart soar to mean that much to someone. I'd never felt so wanted, or so important, or so validated.

That tickle was deep and strong in me. The whisper that maybe, just maybe, someone else who deserved it would be joining Reverend Lynch in hell.

I couldn't even hope.

One hour felt like a lifetime as I waited with the suitcases all packed and ready to go, so hell only knew how long twenty-four of them would feel like as we waited to make our run overseas. The minutes were dragging so slow they could cripple me. Still I drifted, thought, stared out of the window. Drifted, thought, stared out of the window.

I couldn't do it. Not all through the afternoon.

I stopped drifting around the house enough to put the TV on once another twenty minutes had crawled on by, expecting to see my face staring back out at me like usual. Only it wasn't my face staring back out at me. Not this time.

As it turns out, I wasn't quite prepared for it.

I knew we were in some serious trouble the moment the photograph came up on-screen.

If you have any information about this man, then please call the number below.

Oh fuck.

The image was a blurry photograph taken outside my apartment, presumably right before my abduction. He was dark and tall…like a lot of men. A lot of men who weren't Lucian Morelli.

I was hoping my letter would have drawn the attention away from his visit but it was only a matter of time. It had always been just a matter of time.

The number on-screen was scrolling.

If you have any information about this man, then please call the number below.

If you have any information about this man, then please call the number below.

If you have any information about this man, then please call the number below.

There were people from the Work Truths auction we'd been at, talking about how they'd seen him there, including my cousin, Harriet. It broke my heart to see her like that—tears streaming down her cheeks. She was genuinely asking for information, but it was her naivety asking, loud and clear. There was no way in this world that people wouldn't know. That people wouldn't see the connection, the similarity between the Morelli god and this lurking shadow.

Yeah, sure, there was no doubt about it. The pieces were piling up around us. The picture on-screen was just another huge pointer linking Lucian Morelli to me.

We were running out of time.

If you have any information about this man, then please call the number below.

If only I had a cell, maybe I would. Maybe I'd tell them something, *anything* just to get them off track. But I didn't. I had nothing. It was just me, with my legs pulled up and crossed on the sofa as I rocked back and forth, staring at that blurry photo on the screen.

I leapt out of my skin when I heard a car pull back up in the driveway. Thank fuck for that. Thank fuck Lucian had made it home.

For the second time today, I twisted the key in the lock and raced on out of there to meet him, and this time I got further. I was racing, rushing...only it wasn't Lucian's car that was waiting for me outside when I screeched to a halt on nervous legs.

It wasn't the strength of Lucian greeting me when a tall stranger stepped out of the driver's side and came after me.

No.

Oh my God, no.

My body was on autopilot as I turned around and made a dash back to the safety of the house, but it wouldn't have mattered, not for anything. My body would never have been fast enough.

I was back up on the porch when the man's hands grabbed me from behind and slammed me right into the hallway. I had no idea who I was squealing against as he spun me around and threw me right up against the wall.

"Elaine Constantine," he snarled. "We knew it. We knew you two were holed up together in some fucked-up little shit show of a haven. Where is Lucian?"

I stared blankly, every inch of my skin prickling as I tried to work out just who or where this guy had come from. He had a scar down the right side of his face, a brute in the most brutish sense of the word. Dark and deadly with heavy eyebrows that made me feel like a useless little girl.

"Who are you?" I asked, and his eyes were nothing but vile as he stared down at me.

"I could be anybody," he said to me. "Everyone is coming for you. The Morellis, The Power Brothers, your own fucking family."

It broke my heart that he was right.

It also broke my heart that I may never see the love of my life again.

One thing for sure was that I was never going to betray Lucian Morelli. The guy before me could do whatever he wanted, but I wouldn't be revealing anything about the man I loved.

"Tell me," he pushed. "I want to know everything you know about the spawn of Satan."

I gasped when I felt it. The chill of the blade pressing against my ribs.

He was really going to hurt me. The sick fuck in front of me was really going to hurt me.

I was a little girl in that moment with my life flashing before my eyes, but I didn't want it. I wanted everything but to say goodbye to the first shot at a future I'd ever really craved.

"Tell me," the guy grunted again. "I have a whole load of people waiting for a damn fucking update."

I closed my eyes as I shook my head.

The whole load of people could wait, because

JADE WEST

I wouldn't be telling him anything. Not a fucking thing.

I don't know when he used that blade on my ribs. My senses were swimming as I first felt the stab of pain slice my skin through the fabric of the shirt on me, and my squeals sounded distant. Distant and scary enough that my legs were like Jell-O.

I just prayed with every part of my fucked-up little soul that on some weird level, I'd get at least one chance to see the love of my life again.

Please God. Please just one more glance at Lucian Morelli.

CHAPTER SIX

Lucian

I DROVE THAT car faster than I'd ever driven a car in my life as I sped my way back toward Bishop's Landing.

The pieces were tumbling, a mess so churned that I had no idea who was coming from where anymore, only that they were all heading in one direction. Ours.

People had been talking—Constantines and Power Brothers, and my own family on the sidelines.

We were doomed. I was just begging to the universe that I'd reach Elaine before anyone else did, and before anyone reached me en route.

I hadn't known just how visible my own little shack in the wilderness had been to those around me. Naivety on my part.

Please God, let me reach her.

My wheels were spinning on gravel when I reached the driveway, and my heart was spinning to match when I saw the red car already parked up by our porch.

Holy fuck, they were here for her.

There was no point trying to be quiet or calm, so I didn't. I burst through the door consumed with a whole other league of rage and fear than I'd felt before, and there he was, some disgusting piece of shit with his hand around my sweetheart's throat, his face right up in hers.

And his blade against her rib cage, hurting her. Hurting her bad.

The guy thought he was some kind of professional killer, all set to bargain with me or battle information right out of me, only I didn't give him even a second of a chance before I launched myself right at him and shunted him down to the floor.

I was a beast possessed with hatred and rage, no longer caring if he took me out for the count, just so long as my Elaine was free from him.

"Run!" I yelled at her, as I fought with that cunt, but she didn't move, paralyzed, her blood visible even through my shirt on her chest.

"RUN!" I yelled again, but it was the man underneath me who responded with action, trying his best to seize control.

Luckily, thank holy fuck, he didn't make it.

I heard his grunt before I felt his blood, both of our limbs flailing and twisting.

The universe was damn fucking kind in that moment. Seriously damn fucking kind.

His eyes were cold and dying as I twisted his blade even further into his ribs. I felt a whirr of satisfaction seeing that—seeing his payback for trying to hurt my woman with the same callous intent.

His stare was already void and numb when Elaine finally found motion and dropped to the hallway floor. I reached for her and she went straight into my arms, and she was hurting enough to be trembling and crying, the blood on her chest enough to redden my fingers.

"You saved me," she managed to whisper, and I wished it was skill and intent more than luck that had led me back to her in time.

I'd been a fool to hit the golf course. An absolute fool to believe we were in anything other than a web of people out for our blood, all coming at us with different whispers.

"You saved me, Lucian," Elaine whispered again, and I tugged the shirt from her ribs enough to realize she was right.

She was hurt and bleeding, but she wasn't in danger of bleeding out, not entirely. Still, it was enough to have me reeling, sick and desperate, and I knew then that I'd never be able to stand seeing my beautiful baby girl take any pain from any piece of shit in this world. Especially not because of me.

The knowledge that I'd brought her to this was a hammerblow to my chest, heavy and hard.

The body on the floor next to us was just another example of not giving a fuck for anyone's life other than ours as I got to my feet and lifted her to hers.

I carried her through to the bathroom and found my medical supplies, wrapping her up tight in a bandage.

She whimpered but let me touch her, giving me control over her body, even through her pain and tears.

There was no doubt about it when I saw that wound of hers in the cold hard light—he would have killed her.

There was no doubt about the coming truth, either. They would be coming right back in for round two, and it would be soon. Really damn soon. We needed to get out of there as quickly as we possibly could.

"You packed?" I asked and she managed a nod.

"Yes, I packed."

"Let's do it, then," I said. "We're on the fucking run."

CHAPTER SEVEN

Elaine

EVEN NOW, IN pain with my blood still flowing under the bandage, I didn't care about anything but holding the man I loved.

He was home.

Safe.

Alive.

But that wasn't going to be the case all that much longer. Not with the pointer fingers coming up from all directions.

My eyes must have been terrified when they met his.

"Have you heard the news?" I asked. "They're looking for you, Lucian! There's a photo of you outside my apartment! That's what's bringing them here, isn't it? They've put the pieces together!"

I expected him to freak out and curse, or at

least do something in shock, but he didn't. "Sure, them hunting down that person is a nail in the coffin, Elaine," he told me as he grabbed hold of our things around us. "But believe me, baby, there are a whole load worse nails coming for our coffin than that. You've just met one of them."

"There are more people coming, aren't there?" I pushed.

I'll remember his answer for the rest of my life.

My beautiful monster was so proud and terrified both at once when he told me, his expression will be etched into my soul for all time.

"Plenty of people will be coming for us," he told me. "But I'll be protecting you and dishing out revenge with every breath in me, I swear it on my life."

And then he paused.

Lucian Morelli actually paused before he told me what he'd done.

"Speaking of revenge, Elaine. I just killed your fucking uncle," he said.

CHAPTER EIGHT

Lucian

HER FACE WAS magic. A perfect picture of shock as her hands clasped over her face.

"You…you killed Lionel?"

"Yes, my beautiful princess. I killed the vile fuck who delivered you for abuse. Shot him bang in his fucking face."

"He's really dead?"

I could tell she was still trying to process it. Still trying to believe my words.

"He's dead. I bid him a fair fucking farewell." I paused. "And I delivered Colonel Hardwick a fair fucking farewell alongside him. Both of them can rot in hell."

She was still hurting from her wound, but in that moment it didn't matter, she was too caught up in what I was telling her.

"I don't even know what to say…" she said.

I took hold of her shoulders and kissed her forehead.

"You don't have to say anything. It was the greatest achievement of my life. I'm just fucking grateful I made it back here in time." I sucked in a breath. "I won't be leaving you again, I guarantee you that."

She sucked in a breath to match mine, and then my doll shone bright and perfect. A tear dropped from her eye and ran down her cheek, but there was a smile on her face. The most beautiful smile I'd ever seen.

It was the little girl Elaine who was smiling at me. Grateful. Humble. Surprised.

The little girl Elaine I was more petrified of losing than anything else I'd ever felt.

"Thank you," she managed to whisper, and then she broke, sobbing hard and deep.

I wrapped her in my arms and soothed the stunning girl as she cried. It only made my black soul thrum even harder. Pride. I was proud of what I'd done for her. I'd do it all over again in a heartbeat and enjoy every second more than life itself. Only now wasn't the time. Now was the time we needed to get the holy fuck out of there.

"I'm going to get the rest of those vile cunts," I said. "As long as there is life in my body, princess, I'll be hunting the rest of them down."

I didn't tell her that one of the main reasons I was choosing the UK as our runaway destination was that the other main members of the fellowship were based there, in their stuck-up British empires. It had been one of my motives—to reach Baron Rawlings and Lord Eddington. A far bigger attraction to me than Buckingham Palace, that was for damn sure.

"I can't believe it," she whispered through her tears. "You did that for me…you made them pay for what they did to me…"

"They deserved a whole lot fucking worse, Elaine. They're lucky I didn't have more time."

I held her close, savoring the touch of her body against mine. She was tiny, pressing hard to my chest, and I loved feeling her like that, so trusting of me. I don't know how long we were standing there, but the sky was turning pink to dusk outside when she pulled away from me. Her eyes were puffy but every bit as stunning, and her smile was delicate in the most gorgeous of ways.

I told her how I'd tracked them down at the golf course and accosted them at hole four. I told her how they knew exactly what I was taking revenge for, but all the while I was finishing up gathering our things ready to go.

"I'd have killed Lionel myself if I could," she told me, and the flash of hate and hurt in her eyes showed me just how true that was. "Honestly, Lucian. I'd have killed him myself."

I was very glad to have delivered her wish by my hands.

Her mind seemed to click back onto our own situation as I gathered the rest of our suitcases.

"Your photo is all over the news. There's a hotline wanting information."

I knew we were fucked. She didn't need to tell me. We just had to pray that we could make it through the hours to get to the airport tomorrow. It's not as though we could even check into a hotel for the night with one of my other fake IDs. We were too recognizable with that photo all over the news alongside Elaine Constantine's.

I got the suitcases ready to go, positioned at the bottom of the stairs. She told me how she'd packed everything she could see we'd need, and how I should check it to be sure, but I shook my head at her.

"Whatever you've packed will be fine."

"Okay," she said.

"Getting out of here is our biggest hurdle," I told her between loading up the suitcases into the trunk of the car. "But hiding isn't going to be all that easy. People will be screaming out for our blood, on both sides of the family divide."

"I know," she said, then took another deep breath. "My mom will find out about my uncle. She won't let it go easily. He's a Constantine and she'll want answers about why he's dead."

"I set it up to look like Colonel Hardwick shot Lionel. She won't be out for his blood for very long though, since he's already dead. I made sure it looked like he killed himself after murdering your uncle. Only that won't wash. Not for long. Not for the people who know us."

"Hopefully they'll never know it was you. Not ever."

"There's that beautiful optimism again." I shrugged. "Your mom should have listened to you when you were a little girl begging for her care and protection. She'd have probably killed your sick fucking uncle herself."

Elaine said something that shocked me right to the fucking core.

"Not so sure about that."

"Not so sure about what?" I pushed, helping her out to the passenger seat of the car. "That your mother wouldn't want to kill a man that was setting you up for abuse?"

She shrugged. "Just not sure she really ever

loved me enough that she would have turned against him."

If I had a heart, it would have broken to see the pain on her face. My doll truly believed that she was unloved by everyone. Only it wasn't just that. It was the twiddle of her fingers in front of her again that spoke words she'd never say. The way they were twisting, hurting. The way she was clearly so broken inside.

My doll really believed she was worthless.

Only she wasn't worthless.

She was worth everything in my whole fucking world.

"I really am going to make them all pay," I told her, and my voice was a ripple of well-deserved hate for those disgusting pricks.

"Thank you," she said, and there was the young Elaine again, staring over at me with a smile.

It was all I could take. I grabbed her hard and strong before I lowered her down to her seat, showing her my full depth of emotion before letting go of her enough to belt her in, trying to show her everything she deserved and had never had. Protection and love. I'd give her both until my very last breath.

Unfortunately, that last breath might not be

all that long coming.

I was still holding her tight when my cell sounded out again, three times straight in a row before I broke away to pick it up from the dashboard.

Trenton Alto.

My resident fixer and my personal Judas. My right-hand man was a long way from being my right-hand right about now, but still, he was trying.

I managed to answer his call on his fourth attempt, grunting out a *yeah, what?*

"Yeah, what the holy living fuck are you doing?" he said. "Did you just fucking kill Lionel fucking Constantine on Hanborough Park Golf Course? People are saying it was some Hardwick guy, but you were there too, weren't you?"

"What do you think? Not that it's any of your fucking business."

He cursed at me.

"Fuck you, Morelli. You'd better be glad it *is* my fucking business, or you'd be up to your neck already." He paused. "You're fucked. The cards are all falling down. The Power Brothers have someone on their way already. Warren, a guy with a scar down his face."

"Yeah, tell me something I don't know," I

scoffed. "I've got a handle on that one."

"But you haven't got a handle on anything, have you?" he said, and his voice got lower. "Because if you're in Bishop's Landing, and I suspect you are, you'd better get the fuck out of there right fucking now."

My blood froze.

"You're there now, aren't you?" he said. "You may think it's a private refuge, Lucian, but you're wrong. People know it's out there. People know it's where you go."

"*People*?" I asked him. "Who do you mean by *people*? I still don't know how the hell the Power Brothers ever found out about this place, so who the hell else are you meaning?"

"I mean your father," he told me. "And believe me, Lucian, he's after you. He knows you've fucked up and gone after the Constantines. He thinks you've killed Lionel and taken Elaine, or even worse than that…he thinks you've kept her. For you. The cleanup team are on their way, right fucking now."

I knew Trenton was breaking every rule of self-preservation and common sense he had in his head.

There was no way he should be warning me. No way he should have ever tried to save my ass from my own undoing.

I stayed on the call long enough to give him a response.

One single phrase.

"Thank you."

I rarely said it, rarely felt it, rarely considered anyone worthy.

He confirmed what I already knew would be the only route ahead for him.

"This is it for us," he said. "From this moment on, I'm on team Morelli. They'll take my life if I'm not. They'll take Lucinda's life, too. If they tell me to come for you, I'll be coming for you."

Lucinda was his little baby girl. Four years old.

"I know," I told him.

"Goodbye, Lucian," he said.

And then he hung up.

CHAPTER NINE

Elaine

I T WAS BAD and I knew it.

"We need to go," he said. "Now. People are already on their way."

I nodded, mute, praying I'd packed everything we needed to take, only there was nothing for me to be taking. I had nothing here.

Nothing except Lucian Morelli.

It seemed Lucian forgot he did have things left to pack up, though. I should have waited in the car, holding my wound tight in my bandage, but I couldn't do it. I couldn't stay still. He was already in the kitchen when I joined him, pulling the panel from the bottom of one of the cabinets, then pulling out several cases to follow. He opened them up one by one to check the contents, quick and sharp. Cash. Lots of cash. Several guns came out after them in a case of their own.

He was a machine as he headed outside and loaded up the trunk with the final contents ready to roll. I would have helped him, but I was too busy getting my feet into my high heels with trembling fingers, managing a surprising amount given the pain I was in.

"Stop it, Elaine," he said when he stepped back in to join me. "Let me do this for you. I was going to help you into this before we left, I just wanted you as safe as possible in the damn fucking car."

I was startled as he dropped his cell onto the porch step and smashed the hell out of it with his boot heel. It was a trashed wreck as he tossed it into the bushes at the side of the house.

"Don't use that thing again," he said. "It'll be a beacon."

The car was already started up when he slid me back into the passenger seat and fastened me in for the second time.

The tires screeched against the driveway as he sped away, and I stared at the house in the rearview with a strange pang of homesickness in my belly. Yeah. This place had been the closest thing to a home I'd ever known.

The roads were quiet, but he veered off onto

even quieter ones. Rural, remote and out of sight of any kind of main highway.

"Who's on the way?" I asked him when his driving slowed down a little.

"It's my own family coming for me this time," he said, "I'm now my father's enemy, not his son."

I felt awful for him.

"Sorry," rolled off my tongue without a thought.

He looked right at me.

"You have nothing to be sorry for, sweetheart. I have no regrets and you have nothing to take accountability for."

"Still," I said. "I'm sorry."

I had no idea where we were headed until signs for the city showed up and told me directly. I had no idea what the plan was, or where we were going to end up, not until Lucian pulled another surprise out for me.

"I'm trusting your friend Jemma isn't back from her world-saving mission yet?"

I spun in my seat to face him, taken aback he even remembered her name. Jemma. My friend who gave me her apartment keys whenever she was on a charity project or a protest drive somewhere. The friend whose apartment Lucian had followed me to downtown and threatened to kill me in her kitchen. Only he hadn't. He'd walked away and left me bleeding from my own self-harm on her living room carpet.

"Yeah, she'll be away for weeks," I said.

"Good. I have a set of keys to her apartment that I had made up, we'll wait it out there overnight."

It was another shocker for me.

"You have keys to her apartment?"

He smirked, even through his tension. "Yes. I have keys to her apartment. I was planning on using it to finish you off in. Trenton Alto made them for me."

I smirked back. "Life works out pretty damn weirdly sometimes, doesn't it?"

"Yes," he said. "It sure does."

Gaol Street was barely more than a dive, and definitely nowhere that people would ever come looking for Lucian Morelli. He ditched the car a few blocks away in an underground parking lot, as far into the shadows as he could, and then he took the suitcases from the trunk. He couldn't carry all of them, so I took hold of the cash. It felt so bizarre to be carrying that much money in my hands. Bizarre and painful, even though I was lucky enough that the wound from the blade didn't seem to be nearly as bad as I was fearing.

Painful but manageable. Torment, not quite torture.

Together we made our way over to Jemma's place. I was teetering with every step, heels feeling crazy. I must have looked absurd, dressed in a long shirt and one of Lucian's jackets with stilettos on my feet.

Sure enough, Lucian had keys to Jemma's place. He looked up and down the street before he let us into the apartment block, but it seemed there was nobody around.

I was so used to being in this place that the hallway actually felt relaxing as we made our way along to apartment seven. I took the key from Lucian and let us inside, and there we were, back at one of the very first places we first truly crossed paths.

I still remembered him being there, pinning me to the kitchen countertop.

Holy hell, how I wanted him to do it again. Even though I had a slice to my chest, I still wanted Lucian to take me.

We dropped the cases down in the living room, then I headed into the kitchen. I took two mugs out, staring at him afresh all over again as he stepped out into the hallway. It didn't matter how many times I looked at the man I adored, he still took my breath away.

He looked bigger than ever as he stood looking at Jemma's whale tapestry up on the wall. His hair looked darker and slicker, and his eyes looked fiercer, and his stance was more powerful than I'd ever known.

Yes. He was the man I was destined to be with. I could feel it with every breath, right into my heart. Romeo and Juliet had nothing on us. We were as soul bound as it would ever be possible to be.

Lucian gestured to the bedroom.

"This may solve another issue at least," he said. "You might leave this place with some clothes that actually fit you."

He was right on that. Jemma was almost exactly the same size as me.

"Yeah," I said. "I can pack a suitcase of her stuff. Or try to, at least."

Making us coffee gave me tingles, reminding me so much of the first time in that space together. He stepped up close to take his mug and I couldn't fight the waves of shivers rushing through me. Only this time they were good shivers. This time they were shivers because I was so desperate for his touch.

"I'm going to redo your bandage later," he told me. "I was lucky to reach you. An inch deeper and we'd have been on totally different ground."

I loved how he cared, but my mind was somewhere else in its thoughts, along with my body needing more.

It was me who grabbed him, using all of my weight to pin him against the counter. His mug went clattering out of his hand and smashed on the floor at the same time as my mouth smashed against his.

I wasn't in charge of the kiss all that long before he grabbed me tight and hoisted me up against him. My legs wrapped around his waist and he carried me through to Jemma's bedroom, my mouth hot and hungry on his through every step.

I was ready when he dropped me down onto the bed, propping myself up on my elbows as he shrugged his jacket from his shoulders and tugged his golf sweater up and over his head.

There he was. My beautiful monster.

His abs were sculpted from the divine, and the V of his hips was magical as his pants and boxers were kicked off. His cock was…hard.

Very, very hard.

He moved his hand up and down the length as he stared down at me.

"I've reached just about the limit of how long I can go without burying myself all the fucking way inside you," he said, but his mouth wasn't about that. His mouth was about peppering kisses around my pain.

"That's good, then. Because I've reached just about the limit of how long I can go without you burying yourself all the way inside me," I replied.

"You're the prettiest little thing in creation, you know that?" he asked me, and I felt myself glowing, even through the hurt.

My heart was racing as he dropped himself onto the mattress and climbed on top of me, stalking me slowly, like a tiger on the hunt. A very careful tiger. Skilled and caring, even through his dark needs.

I had needs too. Urgent ones. Ones that made me feel alive when my death had threatened so hard.

We were both ready for it, bodies responding on perfect instinct as our flesh worked together to find our rhythm. It was primal and raw, no kissing or teasing. Nothing but the grind of his cock against my clit until I cried out, and then the pound of him slamming his way right inside me.

Fuck, it was what I wanted.

I took hold of his ass and coaxed him for more, more, *more.* He gave me more. He gave me such hard thrusts that they hurt as well as made me squirm for more. I liked both, pain and pleasure intertwined. I wanted to feel owned, taken, controlled. I wanted to feel like my body was crying out for more and less, both at once.

It cried out for both. Loudly.

Lucian Morelli fucked me like a demon, grunting like a beast with every slam of his hips.

My thighs were spread wide, taking everything, back arched as far as it would go to buck for more, bandage holding.

As always, the master of surprises made me cry out in shock as he pulled out of me far enough to flip me over onto my front, again being careful enough to knock me aback with his skill.

His chest pressed to my back, a slab of iron and strength. His breath was a hiss in my ear as I felt his cock pressing hard against the crack of my ass.

"Take it," he growled at me. "Take it like the very good girl you're learning to be."

I knew what he was talking about. I braced myself, teeth clenched as he gave it to me.

I took it, like the very good girl he was teaching me to be.

I took Lucian Morelli's huge swollen cock in my ass in one single thrust with a guttural groan from the back of my throat but not even a single expletive. I didn't need to. My body was already adjusting to hurt on all different levels.

It was fast, rough, brutal.

Lucian's hand pushed its way between my hips and the mattress enough to circle my clit. Fast, rough, brutal to match.

I don't know who came first. It was blurred. Jagged and wild beyond all reason.

One thing I do know was that it was bliss in the midst of our crazy whirlwind of hell.

He collapsed onto the bed and pulled me toward him. I snuggled up to his side and pressing my cheek to his chest felt like the most natural thing in the world.

CHAPTER TEN

Lucian

I WAS ON my own from here on in. No Morelli backdrop to give me control of any situation I turned my attention to, just me, on the run with the woman I loved.

I'd never have believed I'd be in this position in a million years.

I only prayed that Wesley Dale would be brave enough and far enough outside of our social circle to hold true to our deal. Without fake IDs and plane tickets, we would be royally fucked. I didn't have my cell anymore to contact him, either. We'd just have to turn up at the meeting point tomorrow and hope he'd make it.

Elaine let out a moan as I left her side after stroking her back for an age as she lay against me. She was wrapped up in her friend's dressing gown when she followed me through to the living room.

It was a relief to see her bandage had held firm. Chest accepting the wound and making its roads to fix it. Still, I'd never forget it.

I'd never forget how dangerously close I'd come to losing her, and watching them hurt her beyond recovery.

I was also perfectly aware of the fact that we were only at the beginning of our travels and struggles. They'd be coming for us again, and at some point they'd find us.

At some point I'd have to win the fights all over again.

"Does your friend have a laptop or a tablet here?" I asked her, and she nodded.

"Yeah, I think so."

She disappeared back into the bedroom with barely more than a wince and a hand on her ribs this time, then reappeared with a tablet and charger. I plugged it in, glad that it connected straight up with her internet.

My finances hadn't been seized by my father, not yet, so I used the opportunity to transfer my current balance through three different bank accounts, obscuring it from view to anyone looking. I made sure to safeguard my personal investments and cash reserves, protecting my personal wealth as well as I possibly could, even though I was soon to be removed from the Morelli business empire.

I smashed the tablet to pieces after I'd used it, just like I'd done with my cell.

Elaine stared at the cases in front of us as I opened one of them up to check the contents. Plenty of cash, just a shame we wouldn't be able to use the bulk of it. "We won't be able to take that cash with us on the plane, will we?" she asked, reading my mind. "Not without people asking some serious questions."

"No," I said. "We won't. Not the guns, either."

She nodded, and then she managed to smile. "In that case, can I leave some of the cash here with a note for Jemma? I can't even imagine how happy that would make her."

I loved her generosity, despite the absolute insanity of what was going on around us. "Yes," I told her. "You can leave some of the cash here with a note for Jemma. Be my guest. Maybe she'll use it to save a bunch of whales and plant some more trees in a rainforest."

"That's not so much of a joke as you think it is," she said. "She'll likely use the whole load of it to save a bunch of whales and plant some more trees in a rainforest. She wouldn't accept any money from me usually, but if it's here with a note, I think she'll take it. I mean, she can't not, right? I'll say I'm paying her for the clothes I've stolen and the tablet you just smashed up. She'll at least likely buy some more jeans before she devotes her money to saving the planet."

I adored the happiness in her eyes and her sweet little giggle. "Speaking of more jeans," she added. "I'd better pack some clothes."

She was still looking through her friend's wardrobe once I'd finished scanning through my suitcases and headed through to join her. She was holding up clothes hangers and pressing the clothes against herself in front of the mirror in the corner. The outfits were nothing I'd expect Elaine Constantine to ever be dressed up in. Cheap twenty-buck dresses, like some eco warrior would be twirling around a campfire in. Cheap jeans and underwear which would never be seen anywhere in our world. Still, they all looked just fine against the goddess.

It was also a good thing she'd be wearing them. She would stand far less chance of being recognized in the airport with that shit on.

"I'll tie my hair up in one of her bands," my sweetheart told me and fastened one in her curls to demonstrate.

Yes, she looked anything like Elaine Constantine with her hair bound up messily like that.

"If we make it through, things will get a little bit easier, but it'll still be tight," I said to her. "It'll still be one hell of a mission to survive this chaos, but we'll stand a much better chance at least."

She nodded. Smiled. "Pray to God we do. I would love to be staring out from the London Eye with you and looking at the city lights."

The idea gave me a strange little tickle in my gut. A sappy sense of utter affection I thought I'd never feel. Part of me felt like a loved-up little wimp of a teenager, besotted with his first girlfriend or some shit like that. Although technically Elaine Constantine was my first girlfriend, I supposed. I hadn't ever been interested in a relationship with anyone else. I hadn't ever even considered *loving* anyone else the way she'd managed to snare my soul. I'd just used women and hurt women and fucked them senseless as I wanted to.

I drank water while Elaine sipped at coffee as the night carried on. The tension was palpable as we counted down the hours, even when we slipped into her friend's bed and attempted some vague notion of sleep.

It sure as fuck didn't come easy. I stared at the

ceiling while she tossed and turned beside me, every sense on high alert. Only Trenton Alto knew I had keys to this place. I wondered if he'd conveniently forgotten about it, for now at least. Luckily, nobody came for us. The sun came up in the morning and the streets sounded out with car horns and voices, and we were still alive and breathing.

Elaine managed to climb on top to straddle me before we got out of bed. Her eyes were pools of tired beauty as she stared down at me, running her hands over my chest.

"I never thought I'd be sitting on top of Lucian Morelli in Jemma's apartment at six a.m. in the morning."

"Me neither," I said.

She cast a glance over at the doorway. "Shall we turn on the TV, see what's happening out there?"

I shook my head. "Most definitely not. Any news won't be good news."

"Good," she said, lifting up on her knees and reaching for my hard cock. "My turn to fuck you."

I couldn't help but smile as she rode me tenderly…slowly…carefully…couldn't help but fuck her back as she rode me. Couldn't help squeezing her tits hard when she came. "Fuck that's nice," she said, my cock still spurting inside her.

"So nice," I said, stroking her pretty face.

"You look so out of place in here," Elaine commented when I stepped back out, and there was a pretty little smirk on her face, even through the chaos and fear. "I mean you looked pretty out of place at the house, but this is a whole other league."

"You're reading my mind," I said, and that smirk stayed bright on her.

"Maybe we really are star-crossed lovers after all. Our minds and hearts, in alignment."

I was coming close to actually believing her.

CHAPTER ELEVEN

Elaine

I WAS SO nervous as we gathered our things ready to go.

No, nervous doesn't cut it. I was terrified.

I had a battered old suitcase of Jemma's with her clothes inside and was dressed in a way I'd never been dressed before. I'd chosen as casual as I could, hoping it disguised me as well as humanly possible. I had a tight little t-shirt on with *be the world's best friend* on it in scrawly script under a big loose green sweater, and faded jeans that fit me just fine. Her sneakers were okay on my feet, besides being a little bit big. It would do okay. I hoped so anyway.

I appeared nothing like my usual self with my hair scraped up into one of her hair bands, and that was a good thing.

Lucian nodded his approval. "You make that

look damn fine."

"Thanks," I said, then took a solid look at him. He was in by far the most casual combination he was able to muster from the clothes I'd packed for him. He was wearing some loose joggers with a sports sweater on over the top. Unfortunately, his head still looked very, very much like Lucian Morelli, the sculpted god.

I just hoped they'd let him on that plane without realizing.

"Just a few hours left," he told me, but I already knew that. I was counting down every minute.

He gestured to the cash cases on the living room floor. "Take what you want for your friend, just make sure we have plenty left for our airport deal."

As soon as I opened the case, I realized that his idea of leaving some money for Jemma and my idea of leaving some money for Jemma were very, very different things. A couple of little bundles would easily be enough to make her faint in shock.

The letter I wrote for her brought a tear to my eye.

Be you, forever, because you are amazing. Just a shame I won't be able to share that forever with you. You've been such an important friend to me. I'll miss you for all time.

Love, Elaine.

P.S. Use the money to save the planet if you want to, but use it to save your wardrobe, too.

Oh, and please at least allow yourself some little treats before you donate it all to charity.

P.P.S. I've included another little pile for Tristan, too. If you could please pass it on to him, I'd be grateful.

Lucian scanned my letter as I put it on the kitchen countertop along with the six bundles of cash.

"Wow," I said as he reached into a cash case and pulled out another two bundles, placing them next to the others.

"I know these people mean a lot to you. I'm sure the money will mean a lot to them."

I would have never expected the Morelli monster to be so generous. Even now, after all the shockers I'd witnessed from him, this was one of the biggest.

Clearly he could see that. He brushed it aside like it was nothing.

"We can't take the cash anyway, Elaine. It's hardly me being Mr. Compassionate."

But it was.

Lucian sure was turning out to be Mr. Compassionate to me.

Slowly but surely the minutes ticked by. The afternoon matured until it was ripe for us to leave, and there we were, gathering our pitiful excuses for belongings ready to go.

I cast one last look around the place before we stepped out into the hallway, then I locked up behind us.

I kissed my fingers and pressed them to the door. "See you later, Jemma," I whispered, and then I followed Lucian down the corridor.

The street was pretty busy when we headed outside and began our walk. The taxi stand was a few blocks away and luckily we got there just fine without anyone shooting us too much of a glance—or actually shooting us.

The cab driver was barely interested in us when we slipped into the back seat.

"JFK," Lucian said and he gave us a nod.

"Sure."

We didn't speak in the cab, just stared out of

the windows. My heart was thumping scared as NYC hustled and bustled outside. This was real. Definite. We really were on the run, and they really were coming after us from every direction.

Lucian directed the driver to one of the furthest parking lots from the airport hub, and handed him his fare with a grunt of *thanks.*

The driver didn't even help us with our luggage, just popped the trunk for us to take them. He sped away without another word.

"Wesley Dale should be here soon," Lucian told me, then checked his watch. "Next few minutes."

"Is he the guy getting us out of here?"

"Yes. He's the guy who *should* be getting us out of here, provided he hasn't turned into too much of a pussy to go through with the deal."

I couldn't hold back the question. "And what if he *is* too much of a pussy to go through with the deal?"

Lucian's face was deadpan. "Then we're fucked. Dead and buried."

I nodded. "Okay, I just hope he isn't a pussy, then."

"So do I."

Luckily Wesley Dale *wasn't* too much of a pussy to go through with the deal. A black car pulled up ahead of us and reversed into a parking space up close.

"Here he is," Lucian said, and closed the distance.

I watched the guy get out of the driver's side and he looked...agitated. His eyes were roving all around before he pulled a little black briefcase from the passenger seat and placed it down on the hood.

"Is this everything?" I heard Lucian say to him. "IDs, passports, plane tickets?"

"Yeah," he said. "Everything."

Lucian opened the briefcase and flicked through the contents. He nodded. "Good."

The guy leaned against the car and folded his arms across his chest. "Yeah, fucking good and fucking harder than you said it would be. You know you're the most wanted guy on the planet right now, by both your family and the world chasing down that man?"

"I'm well aware of that. Just as well, a business deal is a business deal, isn't it?"

That's when the guy reached out and closed the briefcase in front of him. I could hear his voice loud and clear when he spoke next. "See that car over there?" He gestured to one a few bays down. "They are here with me. Any move toward me and they're set to take action. They'll shoot you *and* turn you in."

I could see the rage in Lucian's eyes. "Right," he said. "So let's get down to it. What the fuck do you want?"

"I want two hundred and fifty thousand more," the guy announced. "Or I'll turn you in myself right now."

Lucian's voice was as angry as his face. "You want two hundred and fifty extra for two sets of fucking IDs, some plane tickets and a pair of fucking glasses?"

The guy shrugged. "Your call, what's it gonna be? You know everyone is after you, just as well as I do. You pay up, or you're dead. Both of you."

Lucian's voice was evil. "You're lucky I can't break your neck."

"Yeah, I am," the guy said, and he laughed. "So, do we have a deal?"

Lucian paced over to me and took the cases of cash from the floor. "We have a deal."

They swapped cases and the guy smirked.

"Nice doing business with you." He gestured to the airport building. "You'd better make a run for it, you ain't gonna survive long around here. Whole fucking city is looking for you."

"Just as well we won't be around here for

long, then, isn't it? Flight's at eight fifteen?"

"Yeah." The guy nodded. "Three hours. You'd better get over there and get checked in."

I was so scared I was shuddering as his car pulled away from us and the other one followed behind him. Lucian was straight back over to my side once they were out of view. He tipped my face up to his and kissed my forehead, then wrapped me up tight in his arms.

"Here we go, sweetheart," he said. "We have a shot at it. Maybe, just maybe, we'll truly make it across the Atlantic. Just as well we had enough cash in those cases for that asshole, isn't it? He could have billed my father ten times that, just for my whereabouts."

It was only when I heard the tone of relief in his voice that I realized just how unsure he'd been that this deal would happen at all.

Yep. He'd been as terrified as I had, he'd just been better at hiding it.

"Let's do this, then, baby," I said to him with a smile. "Let's go see the London Eye."

Chapter Twelve

Lucian

THERE WAS A new flame of life inside me as I realized how I was feeling as I prepared Elaine with her fake ID ready to head into the airport. I was far more concerned that she would make it out of the country alive than I would. Far more concerned that she could stay alive than I was about staying alive myself.

She looked at her new passport. "Okay, so I'm Penelope Anne Jackson from here on out?"

"Yes," I told her. "And you're sitting in Seat 29C of Flight 181. NYC to London Heathrow."

"Great," she said. "And who are you?"

I opened up my new ID. "I'm Jason Ryan Reynolds, sitting in Seat 37A of Flight 181. NYC to London Heathrow."

She looked sad. "It's sad we can't sit together at least."

"Yes, it is," I said. "But not nearly so shit as it would be to attract attention. They are way more likely to question our identity if they see us next to each other. If anyone finds us before we are off on our own in London, then we're done for."

"Yeah, I know," she replied, and gave a cute little shrug.

I unzipped her friend's battered old suitcase and put a few of our remaining bundles of cash in there amongst her clothes. I'd already ditched my weaponry in the trash and wrapped my own bundles of cash up in my own suitcase. Now that we were truly ready to go, I felt uncomfortably vulnerable.

I fucking hated feeling vulnerable.

"If I don't make it through," I told her. "You get to London and you carry on as long as you can, with or without me."

Her perfect blue eyes were so fucking scared. "But I don't want to make it through without you," she said. "I'd rather die alongside you than exist apart."

"That's a beautiful thing to say, Elaine, but regardless. You get to London and you carry on."

I knew from her expression that she had no intention of doing that.

"Elaine," I pushed. "You get to London and

you keep going, do you understand me? I want you to swear it."

She let out a sigh. "But I don't want to swear it. I don't want to keep going without you. There *is* no *me* without *you*. Not anymore!"

Having someone feel that way about me was a strange sensation and always would be. Her mouth was so pretty, lips pursed in defiance.

"I mean it, Lucian," she said. "I don't want to swear it. We make it together, or not at all."

I stared at her, hard. I soaked in every little detail of her in that moment and fell in love with her all over again. She did it. She won the battle. "Fine," I told her. "Don't swear it, but please do think about running with or without me if you make it to London."

She looked as surprised as I felt that I was backing down for once in my life. I never gave in. Not ever. But with her I had. With her I'd backed the fuck down.

She was smiling as we began to walk along with the suitcases, and I knew that she was thinking just the same as I was. She was thinking about how I'd let her win the battle.

"Don't expect this to become a habit," I told her. "When I say something, I always mean it. If I say I want you to swear something, I'll damn well want you to swear it."

She shrugged, shooting me a mischievous glance, even though we were both fucked with the stress and her bandaged chest. "We'll see about that when the time comes, I guess."

"We'll see about that when the time comes, I *hope*," I said. "We might not even make it out of the country yet."

She dropped her suitcase on the ground and pulled me toward her as soon as the main entrance came into view. "Fuck, I'm scared," she said, and the sassiness in her voice had shriveled up and gone. "Once we head in there, that's it. We make it or we don't, don't we?"

I dropped my suitcases on the ground and held her tight. As tight as I dared through her healing wound. "We'll make it," I told her, wishing I was as sure as I sounded. "Tomorrow evening we'll be on the other side of the Atlantic, Penelope Anne Jackson and Jason Ryan Reynolds beginning their new life together."

I kissed her once, hard and deep, before I sent her on ahead to the entrance. "Do this," I said. "I'll be behind you, just pretend I'm not. We can't be seen together."

She nodded. "Okay."

"Okay," I confirmed. "Go do it, *Penelope.* Go

check in for Flight 181."

She looked back at me once over her shoulder before she reached the main doors with her suitcase in tow, but that was all. I hung back until she was out of view before I put my new fake glasses on and made my own way through the airport.

It was busy, people mingling and chatting and pacing around on missions to different check-in desks. Security were alert but hardly ready to pounce. I walked right past several of them without them shooting me the slightest glance.

My hopes were true. Believable. We might just make it.

I caught sight of Elaine's blonde hair as she bobbed her way through one of the terminals. I kept at a safe distance.

My beautiful girl really did look like a regular airport-goer making her way to a transatlantic flight. I only hoped I looked like enough of one to make it onto the plane with her.

She was at security ahead of me. She put her suitcases onto the conveyor belt for scanning and stepped on up with her ID to the counter while I hung back even more, pretending to search in my bag for something as several people stepped up ahead of me in the line.

Elaine was through the desk and out the other side with her baggage before I joined the line for screening.

My heart was pounding as I showed the same attendant my passport. *Please, just don't fucking question me.*

The seconds were hours as she looked from me to the fake photo and back again. My fake glasses felt like clumsy weights against my face and my smile felt fake to match.

I could have leapt up with a hallelujah when she waved me through and my baggage arrived on the conveyor belt on the other side. My heart was still racing as I picked up my bags and headed toward the terminal, but not as fast as it was racing when I saw my beautiful Elaine hovering next to a seating area, eyes wide as she watched for me.

Her smile made my soul soar.

The relief on her face was a blessing from the Lord above.

I gave her the slightest nod, because I couldn't draw any more attention to us, but it was enough that she nodded right back at me, then dashed her way along the corridor, heading closer to Flight 181. But I held back. Waiting. Praying.

She must have already been through check-in

when I reached the desk, as there was no sign of her in the line.

Here we were. The true make-or-break moment. If we got through here and onto the plane…if only…

The gate attendant was chirpy when she looked at my plane ticket and passport. Her smile was bland, but welcome.

"Good evening, Mr. Reynolds. I hope you enjoy your flight. Thanks for joining Jettison Air today."

My suitcases were gone. Taken for the flight. There was just me now, and a briefcase with my essentials in it, all set for travel.

Yes. Thank fuck. I was there. I'd been accepted through check-in and allowed through to the lounge, all ready to board the flight.

And there she was, my beautiful Elaine, sitting in her own little bench seat on the other side of the lounge, staring right over at me as I stepped inside.

We'd done it.

We'd made it through the airport.

Now we just needed to make it onto the damn plane and off the other side.

CHAPTER THIRTEEN

Elaine

I STARED AT the plane ticket. Seat 29C. Flight 181. NYC to London Heathrow.

I was still in shock that I'd made it through security and check-in with nobody saying a word, but I had. Praise God, it seemed Lucian had, too. My whole body flooded with relief when he stepped into the lounge and took a seat at the other end of the room from me. We were both there. Together, though it seemed apart.

I'd never been so happy in my life.

Other travelers came and filled up the lounge around us, busy with their own business and without giving us too much interest. There was chatter, and excitement, and people busy on their cell phones, while I just stared at the plane ticket in my hands, truly trying to believe this was happening.

Seat 29C of Flight 181. NYC to London Heathrow.

I was now Penelope Anne Jackson and I was going to London. *We* were going to London.

The voices of a couple sitting next to me were enough to pull me out of my trance. My stomach dropped right down to the pits when I heard their words.

Can you believe it? Lionel Constantine is really dead! Shot on a golf course. It's just crazy. CRAZY.

First Elaine Constantine gets kidnapped and then her uncle gets murdered!

Yeah, and you know what they're saying, right? They're saying it's Lucian Morelli who kidnapped Elaine!

Madness. It's fucking madness.

Holy shit, it hit me hard, but I just kept on staring and praying, barely risking a breath since I was sitting right next to them.

I kept my attention on my plane ticket. My thoughts trying to be a mantra.

Seat 29C of Flight 181. NYC to London Heathrow.

Penelope Anne Jackson.

The mantra didn't last long as the couple carried on talking.

You don't really think Lucian Morelli kid-

napped and murdered Elaine Constantine, do you?

I dunno. I've heard people saying that he was fucking her. That they were dating or something.

Fuck knows, then. Whole thing seems crazy.

What seemed even crazier was that the both of us were sitting in the same damn room and nobody had noticed.

I risked a glance at Lucian and he was sitting mute, staring ahead of him. He didn't look like a Jason Ryan Reynolds. He also didn't look like a man who was wanted for murder.

I heard someone on the news saying that Lucian Morelli was chasing Elaine down so hard at a club that he kneed some security guy in the stomach and threatened to kill him if he didn't let him through.

Maybe he really is the one who kidnapped her. They think she's dead.

I was so relieved when the attendants called us for our flight that I leapt up out of my seat and dashed straight over to the doorway. I was right at the front of the line with a big, fake smile on my face as the attendant started letting us through.

"Enjoy your flight," she told me, and I thanked her with another big smile.

I went straight onto the plane and up the aisle. Seat 29C. 29C. 29C.

It was on the right-hand side of the aisle, next

to the window. I sat myself down and stared out, heart racing so fast I could feel the thump in my ears.

I could sense Lucian walking up the aisle between other passengers. I twisted in my seat just enough to see him walk right on up to row 37.

Yes.

He'd made it.

I couldn't believe it when the same damn couple from the lounge came along to sit in the seats next to me. They got themselves ready for the flight, loading up their baggage into the overhead compartments. This time the woman actually looked at me and smiled as she sat herself down.

"Hey," she said, and I smiled back.

"Hey."

Then I did it. I tried it out for the first time. "I'm Penelope."

"Carrie-Ann," she said back. "You off to London on vacation?"

I nodded. "Yeah, I'm off on vacation. Got family over there."

"Cool," she said. "We're off on vacation, too. Been wanting to go since I was a kid."

She got herself comfortable and then she started up a conversation with her boyfriend. I let out a long slow breath of relief when her attention was gone from me.

We could do this. We really could.

In the face of two people literally talking about my abduction, I could introduce myself as Penelope Jackson and get away with it. That was one hell of a blessing I was grateful to receive.

The attendants did their safety demonstration and we got buckled in ready to fly. The takeoff was a brilliant rumble up the runway and soon we were up there, high in the sky and leaving NYC behind in the distance.

Under normal circumstances I'd be enjoying myself, but every second felt like a year as I begged the universe that we'd make it across the Atlantic and off at the other side.

The flight was long as we flew into the night. The sky was dark. Sleep was anywhere but with me as the lights dimmed down around me.

The couple next to me were pretty good at snoozing. They had eye masks and those neck pillows to help them sleep, and drifted off just fine. Eye masks and neck pillows would have done jack shit to help me. I was well and truly wired.

I tried watching bland movies on the back of the seat in front, but nothing held my interest. The only thing on my mind was my beautiful monster a few rows back. Being away from him, even just for a few long hours, felt like hell. That and the pain in my chest that was still hurting raw.

At least I'd survived it. Lucian had made sure of it.

The flight attendant came up and down the aisle offering hot drinks. I took a black coffee and sipped at the caffeine like it was some sacred fountain of life. That was my main addiction now—caffeine.

The thought of alcohol and cocaine abuse felt so removed it was alien. Insane. The thought of *anything* to do with my previous life felt so removed it was alien, even though in reality it was just a few short weeks ago that I was holed up in my hellhole of a world.

Mom. Harriet. Silas. Tinsley. Tristan. Jemma. I wondered if I'd ever speak to any of them again, let alone ever see them. It gave me a surprising lump in my throat when I thought of my mother. Harriet and Tristan and Jemma, sure, I'd be prepared to cry over, but my mom? I never expected to cry over her, but I couldn't deny it. There was a tear in my eye as I pictured the smile I rarely saw from her.

Somehow I doubted she'd be crying over me

anytime soon. That was the thought that truly made my tears fall.

Mom wouldn't be crying over me. She'd be glad I was gone.

I think I must have finally managed to drift off to sleep in the very early hours of the morning. The sun was up and the morning was bright when I squirmed into life after a few hours of unconsciousness, and the couple next to me were already awake watching movies with headphones on. I stared right out of the window and I saw the land under us, cities and roads mapping out the veins of the country.

We'd done it. We had crossed the Atlantic.

The attendants did one more pass through the aisle and I took one more cup of coffee before asking the couple next to me to get up from their seats so I could take a pee in the bathroom.

I had tickles running through me as I walked up toward the rear of the plane. I held my breath as I passed right by him. Lucian. Only he wasn't Lucian anymore, he was *Jason Ryan Reynolds.*

His smile was calm, but his eyes were anything but stoic behind his glasses when they met mine.

It sent my heart racing to see the truth in them, because there was no denying it. Lucian was as desperate for me as I was desperate for him. Both of us. Hungry. Needy. Horny.

Both of us happy, too.

Happy we'd made it.

I really, really wasn't expecting his desperation to overload him enough to catch up with me outside the bathroom. I was just stepping into the lavatory when he grabbed hold of me from behind and shunted himself in after me.

"I've been missing you," he told me, then locked the door behind us.

I barely let out a squeak before his mouth was on mine.

His hands were frantic as they tugged my sweater and t-shirt up and over my tits. There was no doubt about it, he sure had been missing me as badly as I'd been missing him, but it wasn't what he was looking for. He was checking my wound all over again.

"This is crazy," I whispered. "Lucian, this is crazy. I thought you said to stay away from each other at all costs."

"I did," he growled. "But I can't stay the fuck away from you, Elaine. You drive me too fucking wild, and not only that, I'm too fucking worried about you."

His cock was hard through his joggers and I

squeezed him tight, working my fingers up and down him as he pressed me even tighter against the side of the cubicle.

It was him who came to his senses before I did. He took hold of my wrists and gathered his breaths and there was at least some kind of rationality in his eyes this time as he stared at me through his glasses.

I tried to gather my own.

"I'm Penelope Jackson," I reminded myself. "I have to be Penelope Jackson from here on."

"You'll never be Penelope Jackson to me," he said, and there was a whole fresh burst of fire in his eyes. "You're Elaine Constantine and I love you for it."

With that he opened the bathroom door just a crack to check the aisle. "Just a few more hours to go, little doll," he whispered, and then he was gone.

Chapter Fourteen

Lucian

THE UK WAS five hours ahead of NYC. My senses were fried when the plane began the descent—the day already marching on ahead outside. My interior clock was a mess, but I still managed to keep my thoughts together and my mind on high alert. I had to. We still had a long fucking way to go.

People were already bustling into action when the plane touched down onto the runway. The *thank you for traveling with Jettison Air* recordings were lost in the thrum as everyone went full throttle into gathering their things together. I stayed still. Quiet in the chaos. Waiting, poised.

My eyes were on the woman a few rows ahead of me, getting to her feet with a smile at the couple who'd been sitting next to her.

I let the two guys to the side of me out into

the aisle and held back even more, pretending to be busy with my briefcase as Elaine joined the line to get off the plane. I was one of the last people to step past the attendants with a smile and a *thank you*, and once again there was no flag as to my identity, they just let me right on by with a wave and a *you're welcome.*

London Heathrow felt so much different to JFK. I'd been before, and there was always some kind of cultural overtone to it but it felt more pronounced somehow. Maybe that's what happens when you are effectively emigrating. You get a whole load more sensitivity to the new world around you.

Elaine was ahead in the line far enough that she was out of my view, but I caught sight of her again once we got to the baggage collection. She was on the other side of the conveyor to me, and jumped into action when her friend's battered old suitcase came out for collection. I gave her the slightest nod as her eyes met mine and she moved along to passport control.

My suitcases were some of the last to appear which again felt damn weird considering I usually had people jumping to attention everywhere I went, clicking my fingers and having my wishes delivered in a flash. That just confirmed again what I already knew. Being Lucian Morelli with an empire around me was very, very suited to my nature. Even carrying my own luggage through to that damn check-in felt like a fucking drag.

Elaine was already through and out the other side when I stepped up to the counter.

I was steady. Composed. Confident. They let me through without a challenge, and then I was there. Done. We were through border control into a whole new country and a whole new life set for the taking. I felt a sense of relief I'd never felt before. It consumed every breath. Hell. Fucking. Yes.

There she was in the main terminal, waiting for me with that battered suitcase resting against her legs, her eyes alive with a clear sense of relief that mirrored mine.

Her arms slung around my neck when I reached her.

"I love you, I love you, I love you," she breathed, clearly gushing it out. "I've been waiting to say it for hours. Just because I can. Just because I want to. And I can, now! I can say it!"

Fuck, how it made me smile.

"I love you too, baby," I whispered to her. "Believe me, you'll be knowing it soon enough. I'll be showing you how much I love every single little part of you. Inside and out."

Only that wasn't for now. Now I was absolutely fucking exhausted.

People were all around us, but they weren't really looking. We got a baggage cart and walked along, blending right into the masses. Her eyes were darting everywhere as we made it through the main terminal, her enthusiasm palpable. I had to dig through one of my bags to find a bank card associated with one of my other IDs and use that in the cash machine for some British pound sterling, and she was still wide-eyed at the people and the accents passing by.

Her energy dried up somewhat when we found a cab and they helped us load our suitcases up into the trunk. We practically flopped into the back seat as our exhaustion truly caught up with us. It had been a long fucking flight.

Elaine's fingers squeezed mine and she let out a yawn as she arched her back against the seat, barely able to keep her eyes open.

"Sleep, sweetheart," I told her, but she shook her head.

"Not until I can sleep curled up against you, warm in bed. My chest is hurting again, but not so bad." She smiled. "You saved me from that. You are amazing."

But I loved the cuteness in her. Such adoration was the most intoxicating thing.

"Where in the city are you headed?" the cab driver asked and I made up an answer on the spot.

"Elephant and Castle."

Elaine looked at me as the cab set off. "I've never heard of that."

I shrugged. "Quite a memorable name, you'll be sure to remember it."

I'd been to Elephant and Castle once as a boy on my way to some deal with my father. It had certainly stuck in my memory. It wasn't a particularly grand part of the city, which was necessary seeing as I hadn't organized my identity and my finances. I couldn't be too grandiose. Not yet anyway.

The outside rumbled by in a blur as we made our way from the airport to the city. I could barely keep my eyes open.

"Elephant and Castle," the driver said finally.

I snapped back to attention, checking out the street through the window.

I got him to pull up outside a budget inn that looked significantly nicer than it would have if we hadn't so recently holed up in her friend's shithole of a neighborhood. It would sure do us alright until we could get our damn life together.

Its mediocrity didn't seem to matter shit to Elaine. She stared up in abject awe at the building as the cab driver unloaded our suitcases beside us.

"Wow!" She was a sweet little girl all over again with that one little word.

The cab driver was off as soon as I'd paid him, and still she was staring up at the hotel. I held open the entrance door for her to step inside and she was tight against me as we made our way to the reception desk.

"I'm hoping you have a double room available for a few nights," I said to the woman behind the counter.

She nodded. "Yes, sir. Would you like standard or premium?"

"Premium," I told her and she handed over a key.

"That will be a hundred and twenty pounds per night."

Pounds. The word would be a novelty for some time.

I handed over one of my credit cards. This one belonged to a fake ID known as Evan Taylor. She swiped it through her machine without any concern.

"I've booked you in for two nights, Mr. Taylor. Please let us know if you would like to extend your stay."

Looking around the lobby, I very much doubted it.

I doubted it even more when we stepped inside the *premium* room and found it to be little more than a crappy cheap box with a plain double bed, a cruddy little dresser and a budget little TV on the wall, but that didn't matter. Not right then. It didn't matter shit to either of us.

Elaine let out a huge sigh as she dropped her suitcase on the floor and threw herself backwards onto the bed. She was washed out, exhausted and showing it, eyes barely open as she kicked off her sneakers and scrabbled her way up to the pillows.

My eyes were barely open when I climbed up beside her.

We weren't even under the covers when she snuggled her way up against me. She let out a sigh as I wrapped her up in my arms.

"I still can't believe it," she whispered after another yawn. "We're in London. My name is now Penelope Jackson and I live in London."

Only she wouldn't be Penelope Jackson, just as I wouldn't be Jason Reynolds or Evan Taylor or any other of the numerous fake IDs I had in my suitcase. I'd already realized that on the flight, sitting amongst the regular travelers, the thoughts churning over in my mind all the way.

I was Lucian Morelli.

I'd always be Lucian Morelli and the world would always know me as Lucian Morelli.

I watched the little doll fall asleep beside me, drifting into lovely steady breaths with the very gentlest of snores, and I let the thoughts tumble and focus one last time before drifting asleep myself.

Just as I'd always be Lucian Morelli, my beautiful sweetheart would always be Elaine Constantine, and I wanted her that way. I wanted Elaine Constantine at my side.

I wanted the world to know it was Elaine Constantine at my side because I was proud.

Proud of her, proud of me, proud of our life together.

What a shame our families across the Atlantic would be anything but.

That was another reason I needed to step out and take charge of our new place in this world. It was the only hope we had of staying alive.

Sure, they'd still come for us, they'd be trying even as my thoughts were tumbling fresh, but to survive it, and attempt to get them to give up the fight, I'd have to stand strong, proud and ruthless. Bold in a brave new world.

One thing was for sure—I'd have a damn fucking load of work to be doing before Lucian and Elaine could take the public stage in this new kingdom, otherwise we'd be wiped out in the blink of an eye.

Just as well I'd always been a relentless workaholic, then, wasn't it?

Only I wasn't right there and then.

I was anything but a relentless workaholic as I took hold of Elaine even tighter and let myself finally fall asleep at her side.

Chapter Fifteen

Elaine

I HAD NO idea what time it was when I woke up. It was dark outside, just the orange glow of the London streetlights showing through the window. We hadn't even closed the blinds, we'd been that tired when we'd flopped on the bed.

Lucian was still deep asleep beside me, and I loved that. I knew I'd be loving that for the rest of my life. I loved it way too much to ever take it for granted.

I just hoped the rest of our lives was quite a long period of time, and not going to be snatched away from us in just a few days, if people found out where we were. That was another case of optimism on my part at best.

I needed to pee, and tried to move without waking him, but I didn't manage it. He reached out for me before I'd made it off the bed.

"Get back here, Elaine," he said, and his voice was low and beautiful.

"I need to pee," I whispered.

He let go of my arm with a grunt. "Then hurry the fuck up. And ditch those clothes while you're at it. We need to rebandage you as well."

I hurried to the bathroom as quickly as I could while still flinching at the pain, didn't flick on the light switch, thinking it might wake up some hitman sniper on the roof opposite. God this was crazy.

I ran the sink tap to hide the sound of me peeing. That was crazy, too. As if that mattered anymore. I flushed the toilet and had a quick drink from the tap before I tore my clothes off and hurried back in there, stopping short of the bed. He was sitting up, still dressed, his beautiful face bathed in the orange glow through the window.

He didn't say a word, just opened his arms and I fell into him as he held me tight.

"God, I love you," I said and it rolled off my tongue in the most amazing of ways.

"Just as well, sweetheart, since I love you right fucking back."

I knew he was smirking.

I let out a breath against his chest. He smelled

so much of him through his sweater that I pressed my nose against him just to smell him deeper. I loved it. Love, love, love. I loved every damn thing about Lucian Morelli, or Jason, or Evan, or whoever the hell he was now.

His fingers trailed up my back and his touch made me shiver—a nice shiver.

That was another thing I loved about Lucian. I loved how hard his cock was for me constantly. It made me feel like the most attractive woman alive. Even now, after grabbing sleep after a crazy, crazy few days, his body was still seeking out mine.

And it was crazy instinct as I ached for his body, lifting his sweater off over his head for him.

It didn't take him long to get naked.

Didn't take him long to pull me onto bed and under the covers with him, still being so tender around my bandage that he was like a saint, even through his dark eyes.

And it didn't take me long to grab hold of his cock and squeeze it hard.

"I love what a horny little doll you're turning out to be, Elaine," he said, and his face was illuminated just enough by the glow from the window that I could see his smile.

"So treat me like one," I whined. "Make me

your horny little doll."

"Oh, I will be treating you like one," he told me. "Don't you worry about that, little doll. I'll be making you my horny little doll so much you'll barely be able to take it, just as soon as we get you nice and healed."

The pause was magic. Our eyes meeting in that stillness that only the early hours of the morning can give you.

He took my hand from his cock and wrapped it around him, his voice was so deep and pure when it came, when he hugged me.

"Luckily right now, sweetheart, I'm enjoying this too much to move."

That gave me a weird little pang in my chest. Something like a tickle, because it felt so nice. To be wanted by someone so much that they just wanted to have their bare body next to yours and savor that moment was so weird I never thought I'd feel it. I never thought I'd be good enough.

I reached up and took his face in my hands, just touching his cheeks, feeling him right back.

An *I love you* just wouldn't have cut it right then. Even those three magic words just wouldn't be enough.

Neither of us said anything, just lay there together, holding, breathing. I felt so secure.

Protected by the monster.

It was me who broke the silence.

"I can't believe you gave up being Lucian Morelli for me. It's just…crazy."

"I'd happily give up anything for you," he told me, and his voice was so sincere. "You're worth everything I could ever give."

"Clearly, since you'd die for being here." I gave a little laugh. "Hopefully people won't hunt down Jason and Penelope and we'll manage to live a sweet little life."

He kissed my forehead before he rolled away. I had to blink as he flicked on the bedside lamp, eyes shocked at the light.

His face was so serious when I managed to focus on him, his stare firm on mine. I could almost hear his brain ticking. I could see his mind at work behind his eyes.

"This is the thing though, baby," he said. "Do we really want a sweet little life? Do we? Do we want to spend our life glancing over our shoulders worrying people are going to catch up with us and wipe us off the fucking planet every damn day?"

I shrugged. "What choice do we have? We could try to make it great, like Bishop's Landing. We could get a little place somewhere, where nobody would ever know who we are. It could be okay. I do like gardening, you know?"

He didn't laugh along with me. His brain was still ticking.

"The choice we have, is that we don't fucking take it. We make it work however we want to make it work. We be whoever *we* want to *be*."

"I don't think we can be Lucian and Elaine anytime soon."

I was laughing. He wasn't.

He wasn't laughing at all.

"But what if we were?"

It stopped me laughing in a heartbeat.

My face must have looked puzzled. "But we can't be. Ever. People would come for us. They hate us already."

"They're going to come for us regardless," he said. "Lucian and Elaine, Jason and Penelope, Evan and fucking *Matilda*, it doesn't matter. They're coming for us."

His words were bristling with fire. With fight. With the kind of strength that people always associate with a beast like Lucian Morelli.

"So, what do we do?" I asked him.

My heart was racing, only it wasn't fear it was racing with, it was something else. Respect and awe. Because it's the monster in him that stole my heart. The man who controls and dominates whatever is around him, not just me.

Everything.

Every fucking thing in his path.

He was sitting up on the bed, naked and brilliant. I felt like a meek little lamb lying beside him, staring up at the monster.

His answer was enough to make me tingle. The idea was one I'd never have considered in a million years.

"What we do is take hold of London and put our mark on it, loud and clear. We work our connections and we use our strengths and we own it. We own our names and our lives for who we are, fuck our families and what they want to do to us. They can keep their bitter shit across the Atlantic and accept who the fuck we are."

I didn't even know what to say, I was so shocked.

His smile was proud.

"Who would you rather be, baby? Penelope or Elaine?"

My answer was quick and obvious.

"Elaine." I managed a proud smile too. "Provided Penelope doesn't live seventy years longer next to Jason's side than Elaine lives next to Lucian's. I like gardening a bit too much for that."

I was trying to make light of the tension, because I just didn't know how to process it. I didn't know how to even begin to digest that we could be Lucian Morelli and Elaine Constantine, walking the London streets together as Lucian Morelli and Elaine Constantine. It just seemed...unreal.

But that's when I realized just how much power that gave my heart—the idea of us walking the streets together as us. Proud. Because that's what I'd be. Proud. I'd be so fucking proud of being Elaine Constantine at Lucian Morelli's side with the whole world there to see it.

"Then we do it," Lucian said. "We take hold of London and we put our mark on it, loud and clear."

I propped myself up onto an elbow, still trying to let it sink in.

"The very idea of a Morelli with a Constantine is going to drive people wild. Everyone in the world knows we detest each other."

"Yes." He nodded. "They do. So let's fucking surprise them."

I let out a giggle. "It's hardly how Romeo and Juliet ends, is it?"

"No," he said. "It's not, but what if Romeo and Juliet had used every bit of power they had in them and stepped out proud and given their families the middle fucking finger?"

I shrugged. "Their families would have probably stabbed them and danced on their corpses."

He was shaking his head. "Not if Romeo and Juliet had a whole fucking army around them, ready to stab their families right back."

I could see his reasoning now. I could see what he meant by connections and strengths and using them.

He was planning on working this city and all the associations he'd known at a distance from across the Atlantic and forming allegiances in this new world.

I had a whole flood of new admiration for him when I saw another burst of fire in him. He was truly a monster. A monster who needed to be ruling an empire.

A monster who deserved it.

The anonymous man in hiding Jason Reynolds could never be ruling an empire. Not from some cute little cottage on the British coast.

"You with me?" he asked. "You ready to stand up as Elaine Constantine at my side? The two of us, proud to be one?"

I could feel the fire in my eyes match with his.

"Yes," I said, "I'm with you all the way."

Chapter Sixteen

Lucian

I SHOWERED WITH Elaine, soaping her up in a lather very carefully around the slice on her chest before we stepped out together and toweled each other down. I brushed my teeth as she brushed hers, eyes on each other in the bathroom mirror, but my mind was already hard at work, weighing up what I needed to be doing in this place.

I still had my investments and my financial empire overseas, wrapped up safe and tight in the legalities. I had my reputation and my known power, and the talents that had led me to ruling the Morelli kingdom so effectively. Letting Lucian Morelli go would be a crime against my humanity.

I watched Elaine pull out some fresh clothes from her suitcase once we were back in the bedroom. Not standing tall and proud next to that little doll would be a crime against my very soul to match.

I hadn't ever known my soul. It was still an interesting stranger to me. Elaine had brought that gift to me by showing me hers.

It wasn't clothes I tugged from my suitcase, it was the little black book I'd slipped deep between some shirts when I'd been getting out the cash cases from Bishop's Landing. The book I'd always used to record the most private of my affairs, in scrawled handwritten text, safe away from the virtual world. I'd been writing in it for years. Passwords, and ID numbers, and names and connections. The most important keys of the most important locks of my life.

Elaine lay down on the bed next to me as I thumbed through the pages.

"What's that?" she asked, her pretty eyes shining bright in the lamplight.

"It's our future," I told her, and turned the book around to face her.

She scrunched up her face as she stared at the numbers and letters. "Business stuff?"

"Financial security of the very highest order." I flicked through a few of the pages, until the numbers and letters turned to names and numbers. "Associations of the highest power. This is where we'll get started."

"Some of those are from the UK, right?" she asked, and took the book from my hands.

"Some of those very important ones are from the UK," I said. "So I'd best get taking advantage of them before my father realizes this is where I've gone and starts reaching out to them himself. I need to get a head start on the battle."

She handed the book back. "So, we're really doing this? We're really going to be Elaine and Lucian?"

I knew it, right down in my core. Yes. We were going to be Elaine and Lucian. Running away as damn Penelope and Jason would be a pitiful last resort. Elaine deserved to be a Constantine even more than I deserved to be a Morelli. She was too regal to carry any less of a crown.

I smiled at her. "It would be a travesty to call you anything but Elaine. You are Elaine. You will always be Elaine, not just to me, but to the world."

She let out another one of her sweet little giggles.

"I never, ever thought we'd be holding up each other's names as some kind of pride thing. We were born to hate each other's names. I was told to hate the Morelli family as soon as I could understand the words."

"I was taught to hate the Constantines with so much venom it would kill a whole fucking nation," I replied. "You were nothing but pieces of shit since the moment I first opened my eyes."

"Strange, isn't it?" she asked. "It's insane how the universe turned so damn weird and brought us together."

"The universe is a strange fucking place," I said. "Only it isn't. Not when you really think about it. Not so strange as it seems. The whole world is magnetic. Opposites. It's full of poles apart in the most extreme of ways with the most potent attractions. Darkness and light. Fire and ice."

"Constantine and Morelli," she finished.

I put the book down and took her hands in mine, squeezing her fingers.

"Just imagine the beautiful combination that Constantine and Morelli could bring together."

"Let's find out," she said, and her stunning smile was at full volume.

"I'd best get started, then," I told her and kissed her fingers before turning my attention back to the pages.

Dawn was just creeping in outside when

Elaine put the TV on and flicked through the channels. There was no doubt about it—her wound was recovering nice and fast.

She dozed there, watching the screen while I scoured through my book some more, creating a strategy in my mind. I plotted out the most important connections, and what I'd like to propose to them. I considered just which of my investments would be the most valuable assets in this new world and how best to exploit them.

Elaine was quiet, relaxing in a way that spilled over to me like a drug, helping my focus rather than hindering it. She was an asset valuable enough to put all of my others to shame.

I could hear the street coming to life outside the hotel when she pulled herself up from the bed and stepped up to the window. The light shining through her blonde hair was divine.

"London," she said. "Wow. I still can't believe we're in London. There are so many things I want to do here, to see here. I just can't believe I'll be doing them with you."

So many things were unbelievable in our life, it was insanity.

"I need some things of a more practical nature," I told her. "A cell phone is at the top of my goddamn list, that's for sure."

She turned and smirked. "I need some things of a more practical nature too. Your cock is at the top of my goddamn list, that's for sure."

Holy fuck, her sassy little face changed the atmosphere in a heartbeat, charging up the beast down deep in my fucking gut. She was indeed a sassy little doll, and that sass had been shining there in her eyes, poking my fire.

She saw the shift in me. That sassiness turned to that sweet little rabbit in the headlights, eyes open wide as I got up from the bed, still naked, cock hard and huge.

I gave her my goddamn cock, that was for fucking sure.

Her clothes were off, practically torn. She was slammed onto her back on that cruddy mattress and kissed so fucking hard it took her breath away. Her pussy was hungry, and my fingers filled her up, stretching her as wide as she could fucking take as she whimpered and moaned.

"Let's see how much of a practical nature this feels like, shall we?" I growled.

I still had two fingers inside her when I forced my cock straight in. I knew it hurt. I wanted it to hurt. I wanted to hear her pant and gasp and struggle to take it.

"Beg," I grunted. "Beg me for more. Spread

your legs open as wide as they'll fucking go and beg me for more."

Her thighs were shaking as she forced them wider. Her breaths were shallow. Her whimpers made my balls tighten.

"BEG!" I snarled, and that's when I knew it with every fucking sliver of my soul. I heard it in my voice and felt it right down my spine, that knowledge. That truth.

I'd only ever be able to be Lucian Morelli.

I couldn't ever give up being Lucian Morelli if I tried.

Elaine was so pretty when she cried. Eyes watering. Pain. Such beautiful pain. Only it wasn't about the wound she'd taken. That was fading…opening things up for more delicious sensations of hurt.

"Please…" she whispered.

I fucked her harder, grunting and slamming. She whimpered, taking it.

Wanting it.

Even in her pain, she was fucking desperate for it.

I was her lord. Her master. Her fucking god.

Only now we were magnets coming together. Poles colliding as one.

Elaine Constantine was my goddess right

back.

I was circling my hips when I pulled my fingers free from inside her, leaving just my cock stretching her wide. I forced them into her mouth so far she gagged.

"Suck," I said and she did. She sucked like a good girl.

My fingers were nice and wet when I shifted position enough to play with her swollen pink bud of a clit. She was squirming, greedy, moaning for more as I played her like my sacred little instrument, faster and faster and faster.

Yes.

This was the connection that had eaten us up in the first place. The calling that had snared us right from that very first encounter at her sister's sad little birthday ball. This was the reason we were here in the first place and it had turned into so much fucking more.

She came before I did. I watched her crest and peak before I slammed deep and fast enough to shoot my load inside her, my hand on her throat as I took my fill.

We were both panting, wrecked when I pulled away from her. The air was tense and glorious, both of us still heady on the climax when I reached out and held her hand.

She held mine back. Tight. Both of us, staring up at the ceiling. I didn't need to see her face to know she was smiling along with me.

The bustle of the London street outside was a whole load busier when I gathered myself enough to take a look out of the window, the morning finding its true swing.

I pulled out a fresh pair of pants from my suitcase, smirking down at her while she winced, soothing her poor battered pussy.

"We'd better go get that goddamn cell, then," she laughed. "You're going to have to help me off the bed though, since I'm too damn sore to move."

She held out her hands with a grin and I pulled her up to her feet.

CHAPTER SEVENTEEN

Elaine

MY STOMACH WAS rumbling as we finished getting dressed, ready to head out into London. I could feel it as I put my sneakers on and it was so loud even Lucian heard it standing next to me.

"Don't worry, sweetheart," he said. "We definitely need breakfast right now more than we need a cell phone."

I sure wasn't going to argue with him on that.

We headed downstairs and they were already serving breakfast in the hotel restaurant. We stepped in and found a table, and it was a whole other round of strange—sitting in public next to the man the whole world expected me to despise. There were a few other couples eating, but they were all too busy with their food to give us much attention.

The woman who came up to take our order barely looked at us either. She had a notepad in her hands and hardly shot us a glance. Probably not because I had my hair scraped up into a loose ponytail. I hadn't worn makeup for so long I'd almost forgotten what it felt like. I was hardly recognizing *myself* in the mirror, let alone anyone else recognizing me.

"Full English?" the waitress asked, and I looked up at her.

"What's a full English?"

She listed a whole load of things she'd be serving up. Sausages, bacon, eggs, baked beans, hash browns, something called a black pudding, and wholemeal toast. Even the thought made my stomach rumble some more. It sounded like an absolute feast, apart from a black pudding, that didn't sound so good.

Lucian was looking at me, waiting for me to answer.

"Yes, please," I said to the waitress with a smile. "I'll have a full English."

"Tea or coffee?" she asked, and I was still smiling.

"Black coffee, please."

She looked at Lucian, and he was smiling too. I loved how easy and casual he looked here, enjoying the simplicity of the place.

"I'll have the same as Elaine," he said, and my eyes widened.

Penelope. My name was *Penelope.*

Luckily the server didn't seem to notice or care.

"Coming right up," she said, then pointed to a counter at the side of the room. "If you want any fruit or cereal in the meantime, just help yourselves."

I leaned across the table to get closer to Lucian, whispering just loud enough that he could hear me as she walked away.

"You called me Elaine!" I said. "My name is Penelope, remember?"

His stare was so firm.

"I know," he told me. "I'm perfectly aware I called you Elaine."

"But she might know—"

He shook his head. "She barely knows her own name, I imagine."

Damn he was so rude. I saw that side of him again. The arrogance. The bluntness. The sarcasm. It was classic Lucian Morelli.

He leaned across the table to me as I leaned away.

"I won't be calling you anything but Elaine

JADE WEST

unless I damn well have to. It's sacrilege."

"What do I do, then? Go around calling you Lucian right back?"

"Let's see how far we get around London, then, shall we?"

He smirked. He actually smirked.

"You're fucking crazy," I said, attracting stares from an elderly couple nearby.

"You really are a sassy little doll, you know that?" Lucian whispered. "It's going to make punishing you for it so fucking pleasurable."

I smirked back at him. "I'd better keep doing it, then, so you'll be punishing me nice and hard."

We were still smirking at each other when the server came back with our coffees.

"Breakfast is coming right up."

I was so ready for it when it arrived. Damn it really was a feast. I dug in like a girl possessed.

Lucian was quick into his along with me.

"Yummy," I said between mouthfuls, and he nodded.

"Full English will definitely be a staple of mine," he replied, "especially the black pudding."

I pulled a face. I couldn't even bear to taste the thing. It looked like baked shit.

My stomach was nice and full when I finished up and leaned back in my seat. I finished up my coffee with a satisfied smile on my face, and he leaned back to mirror me. Only his smile was something more than just satisfied. I got that flutter again, feeling so…valued. I guess it was that magnetic thing he talked about. Feeling so drawn to someone that you can't keep your eyes off them. Polar opposites in the most amazing of ways.

It was him who shifted us, getting to his feet with another one of his smirks.

"Let's go get those cell phones."

It felt so natural to slip my fingers into his when we walked through the reception lobby. The receptionist held up her hand in a wave as we passed on by and stepped out through the door, and there we were. The streets of London.

"Cab or underground?" Lucian asked, pointing at the sign for the station across the street.

I hadn't taken an underground train in my life. It was limos everywhere I went for the most of it—limos, and private planes, and cabs at the very worst.

"Underground," I said, and realized I was grinning. "It'll be fun."

"Hardly sure it would be top of the list of London experiences," he told me, with that sarcastic tone in his voice, but he was smiling as he squeezed my fingers a little tighter and led the way across the street.

The underground was bustling, even in Elephant and Castle, on the outskirts of the city. We went down on the escalator and it had a vibe to it I hadn't felt before. Busy and British in a different kind of way. The platform was strange when we reached it. The other side had huge posters with London musicals on them. My heart leapt at the thought we could maybe one day go to see them.

Lucian read my mind.

"Don't worry, sweetheart, we'll be seeing plenty of those once the world knows we're here. They'll be rolling out the red carpet all the way down the fucking street for us."

I could imagine it. It made my heart race.

The train was empty enough that we could take a seat together. My eyes were glancing all over the place, trying to take it all in. The accents, the people stepping on and off at each station, and the way the train rumbled through dark tunnels.

Yeah, I could live here. I could live in London for the rest of my life. I was loving it already, even on day one.

Lucian guided me off the train at one of the stations closer to the city center. *Wembley.* We

began the ascent on another escalator, and the
street we stepped onto this time was a whole other
affair. It was busy in a much more, I dunno, classy
way. The buildings were so much more stately
and grand, and the place had a whole other energy
to it. One I felt much more suited to.

That's another moment I realized just how
right Lucian was with our need to be us, as us. We
belonged in stately and grand surroundings. Hell,
we'd never known anything else.

We only had to walk down the street a little
way before a cell phone store came into view.
Except they weren't called cell phones here, they
were called *mobile phones.*

I'm surprised they didn't recognize Lucian
from the very force of his voice as he stepped up
to the counter and asked them for two of their
best phones and some tablets to go along with
them. The guy started asking questions, but
Lucian waved his efforts aside.

"Just two of the best," he said. "Now, please."

The guy jumped to attention like we'd just
ordered liquid gold, boxing things up with a
nervous smile.

I don't know which bank card Lucian handed
over, but the payment went through just fine. We
headed back out onto the street with a bag of our

JADE WEST

purchases, practical mission accomplished.

Lucian was all set to head back to the underground and get us back to Elephant and Castle, but my heart dropped a little at that.

I could see the London Eye from where we were. Its pods visible in the skyline.

"No," he said, seeing where I was staring. "Every hour is essential right now."

I pouted. "I know that, but I just want to see it so much…"

I knew by the way he shook his head that it was a pointless argument. The London Eye would have to wait until another day.

I sighed and shrugged and took back hold of his fingers.

"Sure," I said, still pouting. "I guess I'll have to wait."

I was only half serious, and my tone was nothing more than a joke, so I wasn't expecting it when he stopped me in my tracks and tipped my face up to his.

His expression was so damn serious. So damn sure.

"I promise you, Elaine," he said to me, like he was declaring the truth of a lifetime. "We'll be getting on the London Eye together and doing it soon. Only we won't be lining up and stepping onto it like some pathetic little tourists in these pathetic fucking clothes."

My eyes must have widened in their usual shocked way, because his smirk was magnificent as he kept on talking.

"I'm going to take you on that wheel, baby, and it's going to be everything you dreamed it would be. Only when I take you on it, we'll have the whole fucking thing to ourselves. I'll be taking over the whole damn lot of it, all for you."

I could have cried as we carried on walking back to the underground. Only these weren't sad tears waiting to fall, like I'd been crying all the way through my life.

These were happy ones.

Lucian Morelli made me so damn happy I could cry.

CHAPTER EIGHTEEN

Lucian

WE PUT THE new cell phones on to charge as soon as we got back to the hotel. The room had cheap crappy coffee in sachets next to a crappy kettle, but we made the most of them anyway. Sipping away on liquid shit while I plowed through my black book some more, scribbling down some more notes on my strategy.

Elaine lay on the bed and watched me, seemingly fascinated by everything I did. I adored that about her. Her fascination, so innocent and addictive. It was truly wondrous.

"You have amazing handwriting, you know that?" she asked me.

I shrugged, my pen poised over the page. "Nobody has really commented on my handwriting since my school days, I can't say I've given it much thought."

"It is," she said. "It's like calligraphy. I noticed it in your dream journal."

I raised an eyebrow. "You really were nosy in Bishop's Landing, weren't you? Going through my bedside drawers."

She nodded, proud of it. "Yeah, I was. I wanted to know just who you were. All of your secrets."

I put my pen down.

"You know a whole damn bigger secret than you'll ever find in a dream journal. You know you can stab me through the hand and I won't feel a thing. That's a much bigger slice of knowledge than what happens when I'm sleeping."

"True." She laughed. "Maybe I'll see you writing in that dream journal again soon, hey? Maybe I'll start keeping one too. We can share dream stories in the mornings."

The hopeful glint in her eyes was delicious.

I laughed back at her. "I'd be considerably happier about you seeing me writing in my dream journal again than I would about you seeing me stabbed through the hand again."

"Same," she said, and she was sparkling. Glowing. Happy. Even with the crazy world hunting us down across the Atlantic.

I checked the cell phones on the bedside table.

They were charged and ready to go.

I handed Elaine hers and she swiped the screen, setting up the Wi-Fi. I had much more important things to be doing than browsing the internet. I got to my feet and began pacing as I made my very first phone call.

The words were a relief as soon as they rolled off my tongue.

"This is Lucian Morelli calling."

My introduction was met with every scrap of respect I expected. Yes. The London world was ready for me. Ready and waiting.

Every contact that I reached out to was eager to meet up with me. The highest echelons of the underworld and the shiny businessmen standing tall over them were eager to hear my news and my proposals for partnerships. Or at least they seemed to be.

Elaine was staring at me when I put my cell down after my first round of calls. Her own cell was still in her hands, and she was playing some cute little game on there that made me smile. But there was an enthusiastic innocence shining out of her.

"Sounded like it went well," she commented, and I nodded.

"Very well," I confirmed. "My first meeting is

later today, in just a few hours. A very important one."

Her innocence turned to nervousness.

"You're meeting up with people today? These people…are they safe?"

"I'll soon find out," I told her, and I was already choosing smarter clothes from my suitcase.

Her fingers were twiddling in front of her, cell phone forgotten as I buttoned up my fitted shirt.

"Who is it you're meeting?" she asked.

"Devon Quentin and his associates, and a business partner he has a lot to do with. George Ellis."

"And what do they do?"

I pulled up my tailored pants.

"A variety of things. They have networks of friends, and suppliers and clients. Both official and nefarious."

She nodded, weighing it up. "They can help us set up here, then?"

I nodded and took a tie from the suitcase. A deep rich burgundy silk. "Yes, they can most certainly help us set up here. I'm prepared to share some of my own business investments and trade deals with them, and discuss cross-country ventures. I have plenty of ideas."

"And they can protect us?"

I smiled. "They can most definitely protect us, sweetheart. This meeting is one of several I've already organized. If my ideas come to fruition, we could be in a very good position here."

"And if not?" she asked, and there was a shake of nerves in her voice again.

They had every right to be there. If I'd been less of an arrogant asshole, I would have had nerves myself. These connections I'd made were tenuous, and I hadn't had direct communication with them for quite some time. If they opted to liaise with my father and exploit my location details as opposed to truly hearing my propositions, then I would be setting myself up for my own demise.

I shrugged, trying to play it cool. "If not, then we think again. Jason and Penelope might be gardening together as soon as they can."

That was an understatement. We'd need to be thinking again pretty damn fast or Jason and Penelope would never even manage to get hold of a trowel before their brains were blown out of their heads.

I finished getting ready, checking myself in the hotel mirror before slipping on a suit jacket. I looked very much like myself as I swept my hair back neatly.

I sighed in frustration and forced myself to take off my tie and roll it up for my jacket pocket, unbuttoning the shirt at the collar to make me look considerably more casual. Jesus, I hated casual. It grated at my spine.

My pretty sweetheart swung her feet from the bed and got up as I was preparing to leave, fingers still twiddling in front of her.

"Can I come with you? Maybe I could help?"

God, she was so fucking beautiful.

No doubt having Elaine Constantine along for the discussions would be another weight of namely respect there for the taking, but I didn't want to risk it. I didn't want to risk her being at my side in case things all went to shit.

"You stay here and rest up, baby. Enjoy the room and your new cell."

She let out a sigh. "This is a really dangerous meeting, isn't it? That's why you don't want me to come."

I didn't lie. "Yes. This is dangerous. That is why I don't want you to come."

She sighed again. "But you can't protect me from everything in the world, Lucian! It won't work!"

I stepped up to her and brushed her cheek with my thumb. "Maybe I can't," I told her.

"Maybe I can't protect you from everything in the world that life has to throw at us, but believe me, Elaine, I'll die trying."

She saw the argument was futile and dropped her gaze from mine. She was shocked. That little girl in her again was still trying to soak it in—the very fact she could be so loved. I could see it all over her face.

Making her realize just how much I loved her would be a mission I'd be enjoying for the rest of my life. I just hoped my life lasted longer than one single afternoon. "Please, please stay as safe as you can," she said, grabbing my hand as I stepped past her to grab my briefcase.

I squeezed her fingers before picking up the case, picking up my new cell phone along with it. "I'm certainly planning on it." I held up the phone. "At least you have this to reach me."

"Great," she said and rolled her eyes. "I can send you some sappy messages and heart emojis before they kill you at your father's instruction, then."

Sarcastic little doll. I'd have spanked her if I hadn't been so pressed for time.

I tipped my head as I told her so.

"Be prepared for when I do get back later, little doll. I'll be punishing you for your sass."

She managed a smile. "I just hope it's coming. I just pray you'll come back."

The fear in her was burning bright in her eyes, so scared.

It gave me a pang of need. The need to protect, and reassure and love her. The whole concept was still alien to me, but so fierce. So raw.

I held her so fucking tightly, I almost crushed her in my arms.

She breathed against my shirt so shallowly, a beautiful doll holding me tight right back. "Please come back to me," she whispered.

"I'll be giving my everything to come back to you," I told her.

I didn't want to run through a big list of what she must do if I didn't make it back. I didn't want to dwell on the potential fatality of my plans enough to go through the fake identities and the cash cards and the funds she'd most definitely find access to in my suitcase if she needed to run away, I just trusted her that she would find a way to stay alive.

I kissed her slow and hard, savoring her mouth like it was my heaven. "I love you," I told her, and then I walked away.

I took a breath as I closed the hotel door behind me and stepped out onto the hotel landing.

My shoulders were held firm and my chin was high, holding my Morelli posture grand and true as I made my way down to the lobby.

I asked reception to order me a cab and they did so. I was waiting barely more than five minutes before they pulled up outside the front entrance.

"Canary Wharf," I told the driver and handed him the address.

"Sure thing, mate," he said, and his accent had a cockney twang.

He had the radio on, tapping his steering wheel to tacky pop beats as we made our way across the city. I kept checking the time and we were still on schedule, but there was a sliver—just a sliver—of nerves squirming right down in the depths of my stomach. I didn't like them. Nerves weren't anything that belonged in my life.

I had already pulled the tie from my pocket and fastened it before the cab arrived at our destination. Venley Finance. I knew it was a front for a world of other lucrative bullshit, and was fully prepared for the corporate gloss once I paid the driver and stepped right in.

Sure enough, it was corporate gloss that greet-ed me. A sprawling lobby with a ridiculously ornate water feature in the center, lit up brightly enough to gloat about its presence.

"I'm here to see Devon Quentin," I said to the man at the front desk.

I still had the fucking glasses on my face and he didn't clock who I was, even in my suit.

"Mr. Morton?" he asked, and I nodded, taking hold of whatever bullshit identity Quentin had given them. "He's on floor fifteen. Meeting room seven."

I didn't even thank him, just raised a hand and carried on my way.

The elevator was as glass and pompous as the rest of the building. The voices were posh and British all around me as I arrived at floor fifteen and made my way along to meeting room seven.

I took off the glasses and knocked one single knock at the meeting room door before I stepped in there, well and truly back to Lucian Morelli as the figures on the other side of the table stood to greet me.

Devon Quentin, George Ellis, and a few I didn't recognize.

They sure recognized me.

It was Devon who spoke first, offering me a handshake which I accepted before he gestured to a seat at the table.

"Lucian Morelli," he said. "It's a pleasure to

finally meet you."

I smirked as I placed my briefcase down on the tabletop, clicking it right open.

Yes. They were pleased to meet me. I could see it all over their faces, hungry for trade deals and associations. "Let's get down to business," I said.

CHAPTER NINETEEN

Elaine

I SHOULD HAVE been getting used to the feelings of abject fear that hit me when I was waiting for Lucian to return to me, but still they floored me. I paced, worried, thinking, staring at my new cell phone and hoping for something, *anything* from him.

I had no idea about the people he was meeting up with. I had no idea what they would want from him, or what the meeting would lead to, or if they'd already sold him out to his father back home. I could only hope and pray.

I flicked on the TV and British news was quite different to the US. The stories were about politics and football and their National Health Service. My kidnapping was just a short snippet, people talking about how investigations were ongoing. Drama, but in no way the drama I was used to. It felt so much quieter here.

Just a shame my heart was anything but quiet as it raced and thumped, desperate for Lucian to walk back through the door.

I guess that's why I did the unthinkable and dialed Tristan's number at 5 p.m. I knew it by heart, like a mantra. He'd been my best friend since I'd met him in his own world of abuse when I ran away from home in my teens, and that kind of bond gets etched into your heart forever...along with their telephone number, it seems. I was justifying it to myself as I heard his line ringing.

"Hello?"

His voice was such a relief I had to let out a breath.

"Tristan!"

"Elaine?! Just...my God! Elaine!"

Hearing the relief in his voice matching my own was absolutely divine. I felt like a kid again as he kept on gushing.

"Oh my fucking God, Elaine! I thought you were dead! Where are you?! Just what the fuck are you doing?!"

And that's when I told him.

That's when I began a whole fresh round of pacing, gave a massive sigh and told him everything, friend to friend.

I told him about how the Power Brothers had been coming for me, and I was counting down the days until they wiped me out. I told him how crazy things had been with Lucian Morelli and how I'd hoped he'd wipe me out before the Power Brothers did, since he hated me so damn much.

Only he hadn't hated me. He couldn't. Just as I couldn't hate him.

I told Tristan how I was in the process of ending my own life when Lucian turned up at my apartment and blackmailed me into going along with him, only it hadn't turned out like that. It had turned out anything but blackmail to get me to stay in Bishop's Landing.

Tristan listened as I told him the whole crazy story.

I finally poked him for a response when I was done with the bulk of it, needing to hear his voice again.

"Well, does that make sense? Do you get it?"

It was his turn to let out a massive sigh. "Seriously, Lainey, I'm just so glad you're still alive that I couldn't give a fuck who you're with anymore."

"You mean that?" I asked him. "You really don't give a fuck that I'm on the run with Lucian

Morelli?"

"No," he said. "Just stay alive, will you? Things are insane over here. People asking questions. People looking for you. People wanting to know why the fuck Lucian Morelli was hunting you across NYC." He paused. "They are saying he did it now, you know? They think he kidnapped and killed you and went on the run for it."

I couldn't hold back a smile. "Yeah, well, he didn't."

He sighed again. "Yeah, and I can hear just how gooey you are about the piece of shit. I damn well knew you'd fall for him. From the very moment you told me about him grabbing you at Tinsley's ball, I knew you'd go crazy over the bastard."

He wasn't wrong on that score.

I nearly leapt out of my skin when my cell phone bleeped with a call waiting to come in. My fingers were shaking in an instant as I knew it was him. Lucian. It couldn't be anyone else.

"Got to go," I said to Tristan. "I'll be in touch though."

"Just don't come back here!" he told me. "The Constantines and the Morellis are about to start a war, and they'll take you out. Both families will take you out. I've had people from both sides asking me questions."

I blustered out a fresh chunk of goodbyes and picked up the call from Lucian with a gasp.

"All good," he said. "On my way back. Pack our things, get ready to go. Quickly."

"Ready to go?" I asked. "Ready to go where?!"

"Wait and see," he replied, and his voice had a dark tease about it.

It gave me shivers of a whole other kind than fear.

With that, he hung up, leaving me hanging.

Hearing he was on his way back was enough of a relief that I dropped down onto the bed, still staring at the screen in shock. I let myself have a minute to collect myself.

All good.

He was alive. Alive and well. Alive and safe.

Thank holy fuck for that.

Pack our things, get ready to go. Quickly.

A simple enough instruction.

I jumped to attention, scouting around the room to pile everything back into the suitcases. Toiletries, a few crappy clothes that needed washing…barely anything worth keeping. I looked around for his things at the same time, but his suitcases were already organized a damn sight better than mine were. He was a whole lot neater by nature.

He walked in the door twenty minutes later and I nearly bowled him over, I launched myself so hard at him.

It was another wail from me, an exclamation that boomed around the room.

"Lucian!"

I had my arms around him in a flash, like a limpet to his chest, pulling back just far enough to check out his expression. Stern. Disapproving. He was well and truly Lucian Morelli again.

He dropped me to the floor. "Are we all packed and ready to go?"

I nodded and pointed to the suitcases on the floor by the bed, feeling like a nervous little doll under the dark gaze of her monster. "Yeah, we're ready to go."

"Good, because we have a limo waiting outside."

"A limo?"

He nodded and gestured to the window. I raced over and looked out at the street below and there it was. A sleek black limo parked and waiting.

I asked the obvious question. "Where are we going?"

He was already picking up the suitcases, still

smiling when he met my eyes. "To Henley on Thames. A town on the outskirts of London."

Henley on Thames sure sounded grand. I could feel the tingle of excitement at the idea of going anywhere with Lucian Morelli, but this was intense, because I could feel it in him, that excitement to match.

I wanted to ask him a million questions, but he didn't give me the chance. He was too busy getting ready, checking the suitcases were fastened up securely before positioning them ready to go.

"Come on," he said. "The less time we have to spend in this shithole, the better. I'm well and truly done with it." His voice was laced with himself. With the Lucian Morelli I'd grown to adore.

I picked up the cruddy suitcase of my own and joined him at the door.

"Ready?" he asked again and I nodded.

"Yeah, I'm ready."

"Good," he said, holding the door open as I stepped through to the hotel landing.

I trotted along at his side, heading downstairs. He didn't bother checking out. Didn't even look at the reception desk as we walked by to the main entrance, just paced along as him, proud, tall and on a mission to get to where he was going.

Yep, there it was right outside the front doors. The limousine. It felt like a passport into the kind of world I truly thought I'd left behind.

"Farewell, fake fucking IDs," Lucian growled and I followed him, stepping out into the evening chill.

The driver was suited and gave a little bow as he opened the limo doors for us. I slipped inside and Lucian followed me, pressing up close in the back seat and wrapping his arm around my shoulder as the driver loaded our suitcases into the trunk.

"Here we fucking go," he said. "Say hello to the start of our whole new life."

I felt starstruck as we pulled away, still trying to soak in the speed of the change around me. I stared back at the hotel as long as I could until it disappeared from view, feeling a strange attachment to it as we left it behind.

"Talk to me, then," I said to him. "Where the hell are we going, in a limo, out of the blue? Where is this whole new life?"

He leaned back in his seat, still smirking. "We're going where we belong, Elaine. To a glorious damn manor house in Henley on Thames."

Even the thought of being in a manor house

was weird. I laughed out loud as I raised my foot from the floorboard, showing him a battered sneaker. "Not sure I belong in a manor house looking like this."

"Not yet," he said. "But you will. I assure you, Miss Constantine, you will. You'll be fitting in there just fine when we get you the wardrobe you belong in."

He took my hand and pulled it onto his thigh, holding it firm as he kept on talking.

"My initial meeting with Quentin and Ellis went exceptionally well. We have many opportunities to discuss. Many."

"That's great," I said. "So, we're going to be safe here? We're really going to be Lucian and Elaine living abroad? Do you think it will be far enough away?"

"Yes, we're really going to be Lucian and Elaine living abroad. For right now we're going to be Lucian and Elaine living at the Quentin Estate, on the outskirts of Henley on Thames, staying with our very prestigious associates, Devon and his lovely wife, Francesca."

He made it sound like these people were supposed to be our very best friends or something, even though I knew he barely had any friends at all. He read my mind.

"It's amazing how attractive friendship can become to people who want to do business with you," he said. "Believe me, sweetheart, Devon Quentin most certainly wants to be our friend. He's dedicated a whole wing to our stay."

I had never heard of Devon Quentin or his wife, Francesca, but I could tell from Lucian's tone that they were very important people. I felt weirdly self-conscious at the thought of meeting them with crappy clothes on and not a single scrap of makeup on my face.

"You've come up with a deal with him, then?" I pushed. "He wants to form an alliance?"

"Yes, indeed he wants to form an alliance. There are plenty of my assets and associations that he finds very attractive. They should partner up very well with his." He paused. "And very well with some of his other connections' assets too. As I said, we have many things to discuss."

I asked an obvious question. "They should partner up better with yours than with your father's assets and associations, then?"

"This is the beautiful thing, Elaine," he told me. "My father hasn't been running the Morelli empire for years, not truly. People have been dealing with me, singing to my tune, dancing whatever dance I want them to dance. Stepping onto British soil and taking control of a new empire isn't all that difficult a task. I should have realized that the very moment we stepped off the plane."

My head was still spinning, not quite sure what the hell to make of it, other than that Lucian Morelli was truly stamping his foot on London, and people were listening. We were headed to a British country manor, with some posh-sounding VIPs, sitting in the back of a limo I only assumed could be theirs.

I sat back in my seat, letting my mind slow down, because there was something strangely comforting about doing that—letting the world twirl around me with Lucian taking the lead. I was tired from all the traveling. Still exhausted at the chaos.

I snuggled up closer to him and he didn't say much else, just kept holding my hand as I rested my head on his shoulder. I enjoyed the rumble of the open highway as the city eased off around us, the night slowly darkening to twilight. We were traveling for over an hour before the limo pulled off the main road onto a huge sprawling driveway.

Wow, yes, it was impressive.

There were perfectly sculptured trees lining each side of the driveway, and the backdrop waiting for us up ahead was a perfect rich glow of gold from the blaze of window lights.

The people who lived here were most definitely, definitely wealthy.

The limo swung around a fountain and pulled up directly outside the main manor entrance. Lucian helped me out of the back seat once the driver opened the door for us and I stared around admiring the sheer size of the place. It certainly had wings.

A man arrived at the top of the front steps and welcomed us inside. The hallway was cream and huge, with stairs twisting up on either side. Whoa, I felt more self-conscious than ever being so underdressed here. The estate housekeeping staff would be dressed more stylishly than I would in this outfit.

"Mr. Quentin will be with you soon," the butler said, and Lucian tipped his head in acknowledgement.

My fingers were twiddling but I couldn't stop them. I felt anything like Elaine Constantine as I waited for our host to arrive to greet us.

We didn't have to wait very long.

"Lucian!" the guy exclaimed, in an uber posh British accent, and he had a rich boy smile on his face as he paced down through the hallway to meet us, shaking Lucian's hand in a business-style grasp. "I'm so pleased to have you stay with us."

I felt shy. Like a silly little girl, out of place.

The guy was tall and broad, in his late forties, minimum. His hair was dark, and his beard was well-trimmed, and he was dressed in tweed.

"This is Elaine," Lucian said to the guy, introducing me. "Elaine, baby, this is Devon."

"Hello, Devon," I said, making sure my own voice was as posh as it should be. "Thank you for having us."

That's when another set of footsteps arrived and the guy called Devon gestured our attention behind him, looking proud. "Lucian, Elaine, this is my wife, Francesca. Francesca, this is Lucian and Elaine."

Holy hell, Francesca was a picture. She was stunning. Absolutely damn stunning. Red hair curled just fine. Scarlet lips and a scarlet dress to match, her smile perfect in a way that lit up her whole perfect face.

"Pleased to meet you," she said, and took my hand.

I was grinning bright, unbelievably relieved in that moment to see another woman with a smile. "Pleased to meet you, too," I said, and let them welcome us into their home.

At least for now, we were safe.

Chapter Twenty

Lucian

W E WERE SHOWN to our suite after the
introductions, clearly exhausted after our
few days of madness. We had the whole wing to
ourselves, an environment much more suited to
our characters. Still, Elaine was her wide-eyed self
as the Quentins left us alone, staring around our
opulent surroundings like we'd suddenly arrived
in paradise itself.

"Wow, Lucian," she said, "just wow!"

"Thank fuck," I said back, casting barely more
than a glance at the pitiful suitcases that had
already been delivered.

I had no intention of diving into that piss-
poor collection of attire any longer, but I had even
less intention of Elaine making do with her
budget clothes for even a single day longer. I'd
already been making arrangements on that score.

I followed Elaine as she checked out the bathroom and she was grinning with delight at the opulence of the jacuzzi bath in the corner. The bathroom itself was bigger than the shitty hotel room we'd stayed in the night before.

"I've so needed one of these," she said, stretching her arms above her head. "I'm desperate for a good long soak."

I turned the water on and she smiled.

"Look at you, Romeo," she laughed. "I didn't expect you to be running a bath for your princess."

"I'll be doing a lot more than that for you," I told her, and I meant it, too.

She had no idea just what was coming to her. Her surprise would be worth a thousand bars of gold.

She stripped straight out of her clothes, reminding me again just how perfect a doll she was, even though the slice on her skin was still raw. It only made her more divine. A painful reminder of how vulnerable she'd been, and how important it was I protect her at any given cost.

She was delicious, enough to make my mouth water at the sight of her. She'd look even more irresistible with some of my bite marks all over her.

We added some of the luxury bath foam, and the bubbles rose invitingly. I was naked alongside her by the time the water had finished running, smiling along with her as she lowered herself in.

"Wow," she said again, and let herself sink into the bubbles.

I stepped right in after her and lowered myself down on top, and then I kissed her, hard. Deep.

Her soapy hands were up and at me, holding my face as my tongue invaded her mouth. This was us. This would always be us.

I flicked the jets on between kisses and we were amongst the force, massaging tired flesh as we played with one another. She was as desperate for me as I was for her.

She wasn't expecting it when I twisted her onto her side and hoisted her leg back over mine. She was expecting it even less when I thrust her forward at the jets, positioning her sweet little pussy against the flow.

She gasped and squirmed as I spread her pussy lips, exposing that tender little nub to the water.

My dirty little doll let out a moan, pressing back against my solid cock.

"Fuck me," she said, and there was such a need in her voice. "Please, Lucian. Please fuck me."

Oh, how I liked to surprise her.

It was her asshole I pressed against, giving her just a moment of realization before I forced my way inside her. Three thrusts that had her whimpering before she took it.

The rock of her hips was perfection. Backward at me, forward at the jet on her clit, over and over until she was lost to everything but the sensations.

My horny girl came loud for me. The water splashed around us as she rode the waves, coming until she was so tender she had to move away from the surge.

She didn't move away from my cock, though. It was her who repositioned herself so she was sitting on top of me with her back to my chest. It was her who spread those ass cheeks wide and moaned as she took it deep. It was her who guided my thrusts, eating them up like a good girl.

She let out a groan as I sank my teeth into her beautiful bare shoulder, taking it as I sucked my mark right onto her.

"Oh God…please…more…" she whimpered, and she got more. Her shoulders were bitten sore by the time I unloaded my cum into her ass, and she was exhausted in a whole new way, glowing with life once we were finally done with soaping up, hoisting ourselves out of there.

I wrapped her up in a towel before I wrapped myself up in one, and she let her wet hair shake down in beautiful blonde snakes, shimmering.

I'd never get tired of looking at her. I could be staring at her for the rest of time and she'd still snare me like a siren calling me right out to sea.

We were still in towels when a knock came at our bedroom door. I answered it with the towel still around my hips, glad to find it was one of the Quentins' housekeepers with a tray of food.

Steak. Tender and rich and exactly what was needed.

Elaine gobbled hers up on the bed, still in her towel, hungry enough that she had eaten the whole dinner before she glugged down some mineral water and lay back with her hand on her freshly swollen little belly.

We snuggled up in bed together, flesh against flesh. She slept like a delicate creature next to me, barely moving until we woke up in the morning with sunlight shining bright through the windows.

I had no idea what time it was, but I knew it was time to be forming more of my allegiances and cementing new partnerships in stone.

Elaine was still half asleep as I got myself

washed and suited up ready for the day. She sat up in bed as I fastened my tie, her hair a stunning mess like a halo.

"Shall I come with you?" she asked, but I shook my head.

"No, baby. Enjoy your new surroundings, and enjoy your time with Francesca. I'll make sure they send your breakfast upstairs before she comes to get you."

Again she looked surprised. Surprised and happy. "I'm spending the day with Francesca?"

"Yes," I told her. "She has a whole host of plans for your time."

Hell, I couldn't wait to hear about them later, but I wasn't going to share them with her. I wanted her amazement to be fresh when Francesca told her exactly what would be happening for her.

I kissed my doll before I left, having to pull myself free from her arms before she tugged me back under the covers with her.

"I'll see you later, sweetheart," I told her, and again, it felt so natural to be in such an easy new world with no fears hanging over our heads.

"I'll see you later, handsome," she replied, and waved me off with a smile.

She'd sure be smiling when I did see her later,

that was for sure.

Devon Quentin was already suited up and ready to roll when I joined him downstairs in the sitting room. He got to his feet, giving me a handshake that was even more firm and enthusiastic than the day before.

"Francesca will be getting Elaine's breakfast sent up to her," he confirmed, and I smirked at him.

"A full English breakfast, I hope."

He smiled back. "Of course, Lucian. Most certainly a full English. Minus the black pudding, as per your request."

"Thank you," I said. "I'm very appreciative that she's going to be well taken care of."

"Don't you worry about that. Francesca will most definitely be taking care of her. It's an honor to have you both here. Speaking of which," he added. "Would you like any breakfast yourself?"

No, I wouldn't. I shook my head with a thanks. "I have more pressing things to concern myself with," I told him. "We have plenty of plans to finalize."

"Of course," he said, and patted my back as we walked toward the hall. "I'm ready for us to get started."

The limo was already waiting outside when

we stepped out through the entrance. I glanced up at the wing I knew my princess was relaxing in, relieved all over again that I'd trusted my primal calling to be so true to our nature.

Quentin and I took our seats in the back of the limo, and our negotiations started up the moment we pulled away from the manor.

I was very firm in my offerings, and he was very eager to accept them. Partnerships in everything from pharmaceutical research to cross-Atlantic insurance deals, right through to underworld arms deals. I had a sense of drive and excitement I hadn't truly felt in my gut for several years. Life at Morelli Holdings was challenging, and interesting, but not like this. Not like forming a whole new initiative of opportunities with a whole new web of connections.

We pulled up in Canary Wharf and the limo dropped us off at Quentin's HQ. I stepped inside, shoulder to shoulder with him, proud and arrogant in my very finest of ways.

It was after a solid morning of conversations with Quentin's recommended associates that we shook hands on some deals and some of the other business partners left the room. Then it was just Quentin and I alone together again, sitting across the table from each other with a respectful smile on our faces. He was impressed. I could see it.

It was him who leaned closer, curious.

"So, given that you have been so forthcoming in what you are offering us," he said. "What is it that you want in return? There must be some things you are seeking that I could show you my appreciation by supplying."

My expression was stoic as I weighed it up, but he was eager, clearly very taken with the offers I'd been presenting him.

Yes, there were some things he could show his appreciation by supplying. Two of them.

I decided to lay my cards right out there on the table. "I want a few things in particular," I said. "Some things that may be controversial."

"Anything," he said, holding up his hands with a smirk. "Controversial is my middle name."

My gut was boiling with need even as I uttered the words. "I want Lord Eddington and Baron Rawlings," I told him. "And I want them delivered to me personally so I can kill them myself."

CHAPTER TWENTY-ONE

Elaine

I WAS STILL enjoying the comfy bed and my full stomach from breakfast when the knock came at the bedroom door. It was a different knock than the nervous little taps we'd had previously, this one was confident, with a real bounce in it. My nerves shot up into my throat as I headed over to answer it, knowing full well it must be Francesca Quentin out there on the landing.

Yes, it was. It was Francesca Quentin greeting me with a smile, and she looked every bit as radiant as she had the night before.

She was clearly wearing a designer dress down to her knees, in a turquoise green that brought out the green of her eyes. Her lips were scarlet, matching her flame hair just right.

The woman just reeked of glamor.

Such a shame that I didn't.

I was in one of Jemma's cheap cami tops over a faded pair of jeans. I felt a mess compared to her, but she made me feel anything but as she clapped her hands together in excitement to see me. "Such a pleasure to have you! I can't wait until Marissa Frank arrives. Just a few more minutes and she should be pulling up with her collection, armed and ready to go."

I had no idea what she was talking about and it must have shown on my face. She tipped her head as she spoke again.

"Lucian didn't tell you? We have both my stylist and makeup artist coming over today to treat you to whatever you desire. He said your suitcase needs the additions."

No, Lucian hadn't told me. He hadn't mentioned a thing, and it touched me all over again to realize just how important my happiness must be to him. He was spoiling me in every way he could, at every opportunity.

"It's going to be so much fun!" Francesca exclaimed, and I had to hide another fresh bout of happy tears that threatened to spill from me, beaming a grin right back at her.

"Thank you, I really appreciate it."

She waved a hand. "Nothing to be thankful for. Two girls together, having fun. Makes my day as much as yours."

I had nothing to take with me, so I didn't even bother looking, just stepped out onto the landing alongside her and let her lead the way.

All the way down the stairs she was telling me just how amazing a stylist Marissa Frank was and how excellent her beautician was to match. She walked me through to the main sitting room telling me about some of the incredible outfits Marissa had sourced for her and just how fantastic my wardrobe was going to be by the time she left today.

"Prosecco or coffee?" she asked me with a laugh as she called the housekeeper in.

"Coffee, please, black," I said, and she shrugged, then ordered herself a prosecco.

It was a strange situation not to be ordering a prosecco to match, but I didn't want one. I had no desire to drink again. It was gone. Faded. Finished.

One thing I did want was the doctor who arrived on demand and checked out my rib cage through my bandages. Francesca acted like it was nothing when they nodded their approval and gave me a shot of antibiotics, wiping it aside like *no big deal*, even though it had been a huge scary one when it had happened.

I was really fitting in here, comfortable, and so was Lucian.

For once I felt like this truly might work for us. Maybe, just maybe, we'd survive this long-term.

The housekeeper had only just delivered our drinks when I heard a *hello* sounding out from the sitting room door. Francesca jumped to her feet and went rushing over, hugging the woman stepping inside and showering her with air kisses. The woman resounded with style, just as Francesca did. She had a flick of violet in her jet-black curls, dressed in a glorious purple tunic over fitted pants.

I guessed this was Marissa Frank, and rightly so, since she headed right over and clasped her hands together, staring at my clothes up and down.

"This is Elaine," Francesca told her, and the woman's jaw practically dropped open.

"Elaine Constantine?"

It felt like I hadn't been recognized in years by that point, and I'm sure I was blushing. "Hi, yes, I'm Elaine Constantine."

Francesca picked up the conversation for me. "Elaine needs to expand her wardrobe," she told the stylist. "Her location is confidential at the moment, non-disclosure at any cost."

The woman nodded her approval. "Of course, yes, absolutely."

She shook off her surprise and gave me a smile of a whole different nature. Excitement and respect to a whole different tune. That's what the Constantine name does for you, though.

"I'd better start bringing the collection in," she said and she was off with the help of the housekeeper and butler, bringing cases and clothes racks in from outside.

There were a lot of them. It was like being in a designer store by the time the whole selection of clothes was unloaded. She'd also arrived with a selection of full-length mirrors, all ready for spin and twirl.

"So, tell me what kind of styles you like," Marissa Frank said, and I took a breath, then began my answer.

I told her exactly what kind of styles I liked, everything from designer casual to designer evening wear. She measured me up to confirm all my sizes, and her markers. I was a size eight. She had a whole ocean of size eight clothes ready for my perusal, and Francesca was joining in with the exclamations as I started working my way through the racks, pulling out anything that grabbed my interest.

My God, plenty of things grabbed my interest.

Beautiful designer blouses and pencil skirts, right through to floaty mid-length dresses, fitted pants and tight little cami tops that put Jemma's entire wardrobe to shame.

Marissa Frank had everything I could possibly want. Bras and panties and tights and stockings. Bustiers and corsets and tights. Jeans. Jackets. Everything.

I was in my element as I pulled clothes out from the racks to try on. It only took one scoot of me heading into the room next door and shifting from Jemma's clothes into a new bra and panties before I felt utterly like Elaine again. It was like a light switch had been flicked on in my head.

Francesca was as expressive as Marissa was, both of them clapping and whooping whenever I stepped out in a new outfit. They loved them all. So did I. I had a new level of appreciation for every single thing I tried on after having gone without any clothes at all bar Lucian's shirt for days on end.

We took a break for lunch, presented with some quaint little British cheese and cucumber sandwiches that I enjoyed as we chattered between the three of us.

It was after lunch that Marissa presented me with a rack full of occasion wear and my heart truly started to thump. Silks and satins and sparkles. Diamante and mermaid tails and backless gowns. Every one of the dresses was enough to take my breath away.

So were the price tags, but once more I was back to Constantine status, on the arm of a Morelli. Once more, price had no relevance in my world.

It was a deep dark blue ball gown that transfixed me more than anything else. Taffeta interlaced with silks, absolutely divine. But there were others, so many others. A silver satin slip which glided just perfectly over my curves. A little black dress that hugged me like a glove. A pale pastel pink gown with a tail and diamante all around the neckline.

I knew I'd be taking them all.

Francesca covered her mouth with her hands as I stepped into the room once Marissa had fastened me into the little black number. She was nodding like crazy as she moved one hand to her chest.

"Jesus, Elaine, that is truly sensational! Sensational!"

I felt it.

I felt sensational.

But not nearly as sensational as I felt once Francesca's beautician turned up later that afternoon armed with a mobile salon chair and every tool she could ever need.

She styled my hair, lashes, and eyebrows. She gave me a facial, and did my nails, and waxed all the bits of me that needed waxing. Then she addressed my makeup situation—making me up like the Elaine Constantine everyone expected me to be, then leaving a full makeup case of supplies for me in her absence.

Once again Francesca covered her mouth with her hands as I stepped back into the sitting room.

"You really do look like Elaine Constantine again now," she said. "You look absolutely fucking perfect."

I only hoped Lucian agreed with her when he arrived back that evening. Only it seemed that evening wouldn't be all that long coming. Francesca checked the time on her cell phone before shooting a glance out onto the driveway through the main windows.

"Devon messaged an hour ago to say they will be home before dinner. We only have an hour or so left." She smiled at me. "So what's it going to be, sweetie? What are you going to wear for Lucian when he steps in through the door?"

I'd already chosen. I was smiling as I stared over at my new rack of items, eyes hovering on the silver satin slip. My God, just to imagine his hands over me through that fabric. The very idea sealed the choice in my mind.

I held it up for Francesca to see and she gushed all over again.

"Yes! He is going to go crazy to see you in that!" With that she sighed and gestured down to her own outfit, smiling. "It seems I'd better select something fitting myself, then," she said, and summoned the housekeepers to take my new wardrobe upstairs while she guided me along with my arm in hers.

"Let's get ready," she said. "Let's give our men something that knocks them truly senseless."

Chapter Twenty-Two

Lucian

I'D ENJOYED MY day with Devon Quentin, it had given me a new lease on life. A thrill. That's the ultimate word for the buzz that was coursing through me. The satisfaction in knowing you are forging deals which will lead to an epicenter of success. Huge success. The kind of success that I'd been bred to create, and excelled at through my own nature.

We rolled back up at the manor in the limo, still talking through the finer details of some of our newfound partnerships. The driver opened the door for me and I stepped out, looking up at the magnificent house with a sense of satisfaction. Satisfaction and excitement.

My doll was waiting for me there.

I couldn't wait to hear about her day with Francesca's stylist. I couldn't wait to see the smile on her face as she showed me her collection of new attire, my princess getting whatever she wanted and deserved. Elaine Constantine deserved everything in the world, and I was going to give it to her. I was going to give her everything she ever wanted and more.

"Dinner will be a good one tonight," Quentin told me. "Roasted pheasant."

I had no doubt it would be a good one. Quentin's chef was Michelin starred. "My mouth's watering already," I responded. "I'm looking forward to it."

I felt so alive as we stepped into the hallway, alive and buzzing and eager to see my doll, but I was stopped in my tracks when Quentin's gaze shot up to the balcony and mine followed.

Francesca and Elaine were standing there, proud and poised together as they leaned against the railing and stared down at us with a smile.

Christ, she looked absolutely incredible.

There she was again, the woman in gold who'd transfixed me right from day one. Only this time she was a woman in silver, in a gown that graced every part of her perfect body.

This was the goddess I couldn't keep my eyes or my hands off of at Tinsley Constantine's birthday ball, only this time she was her to a whole other league. She was now the goddess that I was in love with.

Quentin elbowed me in jovial camaraderie as they began the descent down the staircase and fully came into view. Francesca was also a stunning creature, but my fucking God, Elaine was divinity itself.

It looked like she had a new lease on life, too. There was a confidence in her eyes and smile that made me smile proudly right back.

"Welcome home, boys!" Francesca exclaimed, but my gaze wasn't on her, it was on my siren as she stepped over to me and wrapped her arms around my neck.

She didn't need to speak and neither did I, our stares said more than words ever could. I imagine they said a lot to the Quentins as well since Devon cleared his throat to get our attention, then gave us a laugh.

"You can get a room later, we have pheasant on the way," he said, and Francesca was laughing too.

Elaine laughed along with them, blue eyes sparkling like pure fucking sapphires as I let out a laugh of my own.

We'd most certainly be getting a fucking room later.

I gripped Elaine's fingers nice and tight as we made our way through to the dinner hall. The places were all set at the top of the table and I pulled Elaine's seat out for her, my mouth watering at the sight of her bare back as she sat herself down. I saw just a glimpse of one of the bruises I'd left on her shoulder and that made my cock hard in a flash as I took my place beside her. I could feel her, her whole body, a temptation and a tease in that dress.

The server delivered the meals, but the food held no interest to me. Roast pheasant could go fuck itself compared to the woman I wanted to ravage. I ate mine with an appreciative smile on my face, but it was barely more than paper thin. My attention was all on Elaine recounting her day along with Francesca, gushing with excitement about all of the wonderful things she had tried on.

Devon Quentin was glazing over as his wife talked about clothes, attention fully on his dinner, but I was transfixed by the women, completely captivated by their exclamations.

"Elaine looks amazing in her dresses!" Francesca told me. "Every single one of them."

"Marissa was so, so good," Elaine said, putting the achievement on the stylist and not on the way she could look amazing in goddamn pig shit if she rolled in it.

Devon interjected at that point, putting down his fork on his plate. "So the question is, when and where are you going to be showing these new dresses off?" he asked, then turned to Francesca. "Chessie, don't we have the Songbirds in the Wind premiere on Saturday night?"

Francesca clapped. "Yes! We do! It's going to be incredible! The musical is going to be fantastic! We'd love to have you along with us."

Elaine looked at me, that innocence glowing in her, waiting for my reaction.

"It's in the West End," Francesca added. "A perfect opportunity to show off one of your gowns."

Holy fuck, how I'd love to have her on my arm at a West End London premiere. It would be the perfect opportunity for a showstopper. Elaine Constantine at my side, proud and shoulder to shoulder as we showed ourselves off to the world.

"Yes," I answered, firmly. "We'd love to attend the premiere. Thank you."

"Excellent indeed!" Devon said, and raised his whisky glass. "We'll get you on the red carpet list."

I could imagine the surprise on the paparazzi's faces as we stepped out of the limousine with the

Quentins. It would be absolutely fucking glorious.

"Thank you," Elaine said to them, her voice so sweet with gratitude. "Thanks so much, really."

"You're very welcome," Francesca replied, and she meant it. They'd be really damn pleased to have us at their side at the public outing, of that I was sure.

Elaine's fingers were so delicate as they sought out mine under the table. I squeezed hers right back, brushing my thumb over her knuckles. God, I fucking loved her.

The rest of the conversation over dinner was flowing and easy, the companionship of this couple something I hadn't experienced all that much in my life. It felt surprisingly like a friendship, not a business partnership finding its ruthless feet. It was something I wasn't all that well acquainted with, but I was liking it. Enjoying it.

Maybe I was actually capable of forming genuine friendships. Besides Elliot Morelli back home, I didn't have all that many people I held true affection for. My life was certainly taking some very strange turns of late, maybe this would be another to add to the collection.

The four of us ate dessert together, another fine presentation from the chef. Mixed berry tart, with raspberries and plums.

I was truly done with eating when I dabbed my mouth with my napkin and reclined back in my chair, my interest in the conversation on British politics drawing to a close.

All I wanted was to get that girl of mine upstairs to our bedroom.

When Devon threw down his own napkin and shot a hungry look at Francesca, it was obvious he was wanting to get her up to theirs too.

"I've had a lovely dinner with you both," he said to us, clearly drawing a close to the evening.

I gave him a nod and a smirk. "Very much reciprocated."

"Fantastic," he said. "I'm sure we'll be having many more."

Francesca hugged and air kissed Elaine with real affection before we all headed back through to the hall together. They disappeared off on their way with a wave and a *good night* and Elaine and I were left at the staircase up to our wing, waving them off right back.

And then it was us.

Alone.

One look from me had her taking in a breath, and she was as desperate as I was when I grabbed her tight and kissed her hard, tasting mixed berries and lipstick. We headed upstairs and along the landing, a tangle of limbs and kisses, flesh seeking flesh.

We stumbled through our bedroom door but I didn't throw her down onto the bed. Instead I backed off her, leaving her gasping, lips puffy and lipstick smeared.

"Twirl for me," I told her, and it was a command.

She looked surprisingly nervous as she did as she was instructed, doing a ballerina twist nice and slowly.

The silver satin of her dress was a shimmer, enough to make me heady. Her hair was alive with sparkles under the light.

"You set me on fucking fire, you know that?" I asked her, and she looked so flattered it was unbelievable. It was insane, just how beautiful that woman was.

"You set me on fire to match, you know that?" she asked, and there was that sweet sassiness in her I adored.

My next instruction felt like a crime, but I couldn't hold back. No matter how much I was enjoying the beauty of that dress on her, I'd be enjoying the beauty of her flesh underneath it so much more.

"Strip for me," I said. "Nice and slow."

Once again, she did as she was told.

She let the straps of the dress fall from her shoulders and did another spin. Slowly.

There were the bite marks I'd left on her the night before, appearing perfectly from beneath the fabric.

I loved seeing her marked like that. Owned like that. Hurt like that, by me.

If anyone else ever hurt her in any way again, I'd skin them alive, but to see my own brutality etched into her was nothing short of filthy magic.

My cock was so hard it was fucking painful in my pants when I closed the distance between us. Her dress dropped to the floor around her feet, and she was wearing white lace panties, so fucking pretty. I tugged them down and dropped to my knees along with them, and there was her wet pussy, freshly waxed and begging for my tongue.

She gasped as I pressed my mouth to her slit, wrapping my arms around her thighs to spread them wider.

Still, the insanity of this new world was a shock to me.

I was on my knees.

A Morelli on their knees before a Constantine.

Lucian Morelli on his knees before Elaine Constantine.

Who'd have thought it would be the greatest feeling in the world?

CHAPTER TWENTY-THREE

Elaine

WAKING UP WITH a sore pussy was something I could happily get used to. I don't know what time we eventually fell asleep, but it was late. Lucian had played with me for hours, only giving me his cum when I was so used up I couldn't come for him anymore.

I reached out for my lover by my side, eager to snuggle in, but he wasn't there. I jolted, looking around the room for him, but he was nowhere to be seen.

There was only a note on the bedside table.

See you later, princess.

Of course he'd gone. He was Lucian Morelli. He'd probably been signing deals for his new empire since six in the morning, regardless of what time we went to bed. It made me smile to myself. He was truly back to him again. Only I wasn't back to me. I wasn't the old Elaine Constantine hiding behind drinks and parties and feeling ashamed of herself behind a sheen of glamor. I was someone else. A new Elaine with all the positives of my old self with a whole host of new ones.

And that was all thanks to the man I once believed to be a monster.

I reached for my cell from the bedside table and there was a message waiting for me. Tristan. The only one besides Lucian with my number.

His words were simple.

Call me when you get this. URGENT!!

I checked out the time. It was 10 a.m. It would be 5 a.m. back home. I weighed it up, but the instruction was clear. There was that little instinctive feeling of worry that couldn't be shaken off. My finger pressed the call button and I waited for it to connect, telling myself I'd give him just a few seconds to pick up, in case he was sleeping, but he wasn't. He answered in a beat.

"Lainey, thank fuck you called. You're all over the news here in a whole other way."

The hairs on the back of my neck stood up. "What other way?"

"They've figured out who it is. They figured out it's Lucian Morelli. The gossip blogs are saying he's with you, and you are a fucking couple."

For once the gossip channels were surprisingly accurate. Made a change. Still, the thought that people were talking about it, realizing it, gossiping about it…our families would be realizing it, too. Shit!

"They'll be coming after you," Tristan said, stating the obvious. "You know that. They'll be coming after you damn quick."

"Yeah, I do know that," I said. "We both do. Me and Lucian."

"You gonna run again, then?" he asked me. "Get the hell out of London whatever you do. That's where the rumors say you are."

I bit my lip before I answered, registering just how brazen our plans were to step out together over here and let the world know we belonged together.

"You are going to run, right?" Tristan asked.

"No," I told him. "We're not. We're going to a West End show together this weekend."

He took a breath. He actually sucked in a breath. "Are you both out of your fucking minds? You know they'll come for you!"

Yes, I knew that, but I also had faith in Lucian, and how strong he was in forging our new life here and making it secure. I didn't even try telling Tristan that, because his faith in the monster who knocked him unconscious wasn't likely to be all that high.

"We'll be alright," I said. "We have plans."

"Don't do this, Lainey. Please, don't do this. They'll try to kill you. Run away!"

I sounded weirdly self-assured when I answered, with a strength in my tone I didn't expect to hear. "I don't want to run away," I told him. "I want to stand by Lucian. They can come for us if they like, but I'm going to be alongside him, in the spotlight for everyone to see."

"Then you're fucking insane. Call me when you come to your damn senses," he said, and hung up.

Tristan had never once hung up on me in all the years I'd known him. I'd lost my damn senses plenty of damn times throughout our friendship, but never enough to wind him up enough to end a call.

Maybe I really was insane. Maybe both Lucian and I were. Maybe we were so blinded by our love for each other that we wanted nothing more than to show that off to the world rather than accept that it might get us killed. I just hoped the gossips wouldn't find out where we were headed to on the weekend. The last thing I wanted was to be shot dead on the first red carpet we stepped onto.

I headed down to see Francesca after I'd showered and dressed, loving life in a decent pair of jeans that actually fit me. She was all smiles as we sat down to breakfast together, telling me all over again just how good my outfit choices were yesterday.

I saw genuine friendship in her eyes and craved more of that, trusting fate enough to have put a genuine friend in my path in this new world.

She clearly wasn't expecting me to share my truth with her, not over her breakfast cereal. She nearly spilled the milk she was pouring onto her cornflakes when I looked her right in the eyes and said the words.

"Our families are probably going to try to kill us when they find out we're here together. I just hope it's not in the West End on Saturday night."

She stared over at me for a few seconds before she responded. "Well, yes, I, um…I have heard plenty of stories about the rivalry between the Morellis and the Constantines."

"Rivalry enough that they would want to wipe us out rather than see us together."

"But surely they won't be able to?" she asked

me. "Not when you're publicly declared as together and the whole world knows about it. Wouldn't that point all the fingers directly at them?"

"I don't know. I just know they're going to try. Once we're established in public and everyone is getting used to it, then maybe they won't risk it, not without people speculating it was them with a grudge, but straight up that won't mean anything to them. They'll be too damn angry at being betrayed."

"That's what Devon said. He said the first round of revelations in public will be intense. Likely on both sides of the Atlantic. He said that's why it's been so important to get Lucian's signature on so many deals and partnerships and so much set in stone."

"Did he say he thinks we'll get ourselves killed?" I dared to ask.

She poised her spoon on the way to her mouth, clearly taken aback. "He, um…he said there might be some…difficulties."

I held her stare. "He thinks we'll get ourselves killed, right?"

"He thinks it might be dangerous for a while, but he doesn't think the West End will be the venue to wipe you out. He thinks the whole world is going to be cheering and flashing cameras and screaming it all over the globe."

The idea of that still gave me excited tingles. I so much wanted to be in front of flashing cameras along with Lucian. I wanted people to be screaming it all over the globe.

I poured milk over my own cereal, managing a much easier smile as I shifted our chat onto much easier ground.

"So, tell me some more about Songbirds in the Wind," I said.

She bought into the change of conversation, giving me a much easier smile herself. "It's most certainly going to be a good one," she said.

By the time she finished talking, I had no doubt about that.

I only hoped we'd survive it.

CHAPTER TWENTY-FOUR

Lucian

W E HAD JUST a few days before the paparazzi would go insane. Just a few days before our presence would be known around the globe. I'd already seen the gossip columns. I knew the rumors were flying and I knew that our course ahead was clear. Me and her, standing strong.

I needed to be ready for it.

My web of connections was sealed in stone, secure and invested. Devon Quentin was at the head of a network that would keep Elaine and me at the heart of an empire. I could run Morelli Holdings from here for now. The location was temporary, but my companion was not.

She was my life now. Forever.

As well as setting up the Morelli-Constantine Manor, I was going to demonstrate my love for Elaine in the most spectacular of ways, and had already started on the arrangements, but first of all I had a much more pressing engagement to be putting my attention into.

"Are you sure this is a sound idea?" Quentin asked on the limo ride back to the manor. "The West End will be a fantastic venue to strut around in your first public appearance, but it will be…dramatic."

"Are you trying to back out of the invitation to have us included on the VIP list like a pussy?" I asked him with a smirk on my face.

He rolled his eyes at me. "No, of course not, Morelli. I'm no pussy. I'm just well aware it will cause some controversy overseas."

"Not as well aware as I am," I replied. "I'm very well aware it will cause some controversy."

He'd been looking into US gossip news too, I could see it. It was probably being whispered about behind every closed door in his corporate HQ. *Morelli and Constantine, shhh.* He was probably shitting his pants that he'd be caught up in the crossfire if my family opted to take us out on the red carpet that weekend.

"Fine, then," he said. "If you're signing your own death warrant, that's your call."

I'd been weighing that up myself, and I was undoubtedly signing my own death warrant.

Whether they'd come for us outside a London West End theater was a different matter. I didn't think even my family or Elaine's would be quite so brazen as to take us out so blatantly in public. Still, I could be surprised. They could try.

Hopefully they wouldn't. Hopefully both sides of the battlefield would realize that we weren't just escapees on the run looking for an easy life anymore, we were standing proud and firm, ready for the fight.

At least, I was. I'd fight with flying axes and fists and machine guns happily enough all day long, but my Elaine was a beautiful little darling who deserved protection from every flying fist on the planet. I'd give everything to give her that protection.

We were approaching the driveway when Quentin's cell buzzed. His eyes went straight to mine once he'd read the message.

"Those things you wanted," he said, clearly aware of the driver's ears in the front seat.

"Yes?" I prompted, knowing full well what *things* he was referring to.

"They'll be ready soon," he told me. "Sunday evening most likely. They'll be delivered by nightfall."

I was pleased. Very fucking pleased. "Thank

you," I said.

"You're welcome," he replied.

My tiredness was catching up with me as we left the limo on the driveway and stepped back into the manor. I'd barely slept the night before, but my senses were on high alert as Elaine came charging down the hallway, flinging herself into my arms.

"Welcome home, baby," she whispered, peppering my cheeks with kisses.

Home.

Another use of the word out of the blue.

I couldn't wait to see her exclamation when she saw the home of our own. It appeared the impetus to move out of Quentin Manor wouldn't be coming from the Quentins anytime soon, though. Both Francesca and Devon looked very enthusiastic when the housekeeper approached us about dinner that evening, asking us what time we'd be sitting down to eat.

"What time works for you?" Devon asked, looking at me, but I looked at Elaine, in her hot new day clothes, her time more valuable to me than mine.

She shrugged, innocently. "Whenever works for you."

She was so fucking cute. A woman like Elaine

Constantine could be looking down her nose at any human being she chose to, even the Quentins, but she was doing anything but. You'd think they were our lords and saviors.

Quite possibly because they were. They just didn't realize it.

"We'll see you at seven," I told Devon, stepping in to seal the decision.

"Seven," he told the housekeeper, and my word was law.

Elaine didn't bother getting dressed more extravagantly for the meal once we'd made our way upstairs to the wing. She was still buzzing with happiness to see me, but I could see a conversation brewing on her face. Nerves.

"Tristan called me today," she said.

I knew exactly what that would be for. "Gossip columns," I responded, and she nodded.

"He thinks we should be running away."

"So would anyone who knows the situation and our families, but they can go fuck themselves, Elaine. I'm not backing down on this for anyone. You're the love of my life and I'll be shouting it from the fucking rooftops. Our families can suck it up and take it."

"But what if they come for us?" she asked.

"They'll want to," I said. "But our empire and

roots here are growing and expanding firmly. I hope they'll have more sense than to take a shot at that."

I could see she wasn't so sure. She knew her mother after all, no doubt grieving the prick who'd spent years giving her daughter over to the cunts in the *fellowship*. Still, I knew my father. He'd no doubt be fuming to the point of abject rage, too. My father had a brain at least. I hoped he chose to use it.

"We're really doing this?" she asked. "The West End premiere?"

"Yes," I told her. "We're definitely doing it."

She didn't question me again, just turned her attention to dinnertime, saying how excited she was with her new friendship with Francesca. Again, it was lovely to see her glowing so brightly, right from the core.

Dinner was nice. Once more I was far more interested in Elaine enjoying the conversations than I was in enjoying them myself. I saw Devon smirking at me when he realized I was staring at Elaine between every mouthful of roasted lamb.

Francesca didn't notice. She was chatting away quite happily to my princess, clearly excited about the friendship just as much as Elaine was. I loved that. I adored that. The Quentins would no doubt be high on our list of guests when we were in our own kingdom.

We headed upstairs as soon as dinner was over. As usual my hands were all over her as soon as she stepped in through the bedroom door. As always, she was desperate right back, begging for everything she took from me.

One thing she did ask for was pain, beautiful pain. Only I didn't give it to her, not that night. I had a whole set of other plans on that front, too. Ones I wanted her skin clear and flawless for, a perfect canvas for when I did truly put some marks on her.

"Wait for your gifts," I told her as I fucked her pretty little slit from behind. "You'll be given them when I choose."

I knew she loved that from me. Ownership. Possession. Making her my hungry little submissive under my command.

I made her come, my fingers rubbing her clit as I slammed into her, only giving her my cum in return when she was riding the wave. Fuck, I was spent when we were done, long days and nights finally catching up with me.

Then we did something we hadn't done all that much of before. We lay in bed together, staring at each other in the fuzzy glow of the aftermath, asking each other random questions.

"Do you like snow?"

"What's your very favorite color? The exact shade, not a vague one?"

"Have you ever watched a sitcom and been hysterical laughing?"

"What's your star sign? Have you ever had your birth chart made?"

It was so much fun. So lively. So lighthearted. Something we hadn't had much of in all the time we'd known each other.

That's when I picked up on it in myself—just how much I wanted to see the same things I'd seen in her eyes when she was looking at me as when she'd been looking at Francesca downstairs across the dinner table. Friendship as well as love. Love was all-consuming and everything, but friendship is knowing. Truly knowing someone. I wanted to know my princess inside out.

She was asleep before I was, the bedside lamp still on on my side of the bed. I watched her, smiling to myself.

I couldn't wait to show her off to the world. Miss Elaine Constantine on my arm on the red carpet.

My love, my life. My very best friend.

CHAPTER TWENTY-FIVE
Elaine

I MUST HAVE twirled a thousand times in front of the mirror, staring at the sparkle in my sapphire gown while Francesca stood beside me. She looked absolutely sensational, in a bright orange dress fitted like perfection to her curves. It was so striking. Totally beautiful.

"You look so beautiful!" she told me for the hundredth time as I checked out my back in the mirror all over again.

"Thanks," I said. "I'm just…I'll be standing next to Lucian Morelli, the hottest guy on the planet."

She laughed at that. "Just as well you're probably the hottest girl on the planet, then."

I rolled my eyes, because that was a crazy statement, but it still made me feel so nice inside, her being so nice to me.

She checked the time.

"Really, we have to go now. The boys will be waiting downstairs. Fuck, how Devon wishes Lucian was a drinker, he'd love to be knocking back whisky with him tonight."

It was my turn to laugh. "Fuck, how you wish I was a drinker too, I imagine," I said, gesturing to the glass in her hand. "You'd love to be knocking back prosecco with me tonight."

One thing was certain. I wouldn't be knocking back anything. Me and alcohol were well and truly enemies these days.

I took a deep breath before we began our descent downstairs from Francesca's bedroom. I had been trying my best not to touch my makeup, since it had been applied just right by the beautician. I wanted to look as perfect as possible for the red carpet.

I thought I'd seen Lucian taken aback by how I looked before, but it was nothing compared to how his eyes widened when I stepped through the sitting room doorway that night.

It was enough to knock me sideways. Absolute, total, adoration. I can only imagine my stare at him must have been equally as adoring, because he looked absolutely fucking amazing.

I had no idea when he'd been fitted for his

tuxedo, but it was perfection on him. He was a god. A pure god. The sight of him made my heart race, giving me literal shivers because I was so excited.

He put his mineral water down on the coffee table and walked right over, tipping my face up to his. "Elaine. I have no words. I'll be the proudest man alive tonight."

I must have grinned like a happy little girl, my eyes meeting his with devotion. This man *was* a god. *My* god.

"Time to roll," Devon said and I looked over to see his hand in Francesca's, gripping tight.

Yeah, she was his princess, just like I was Lucian's. It was written all over his face, just as he was enough to set her on fire right back. So lovely to see it.

The limo was waiting outside for us, ready to go. My heart was still thumping, nerves and excitement and love a heady mash-up.

Lucian stroked my knuckles for the whole ride into the city while the Quentins told us all over again about the different performers and VIPs who'd be there with us. I was only half listening, too focused on London through the windows, burning bright.

Wow, the West End was thrumming with

energy when we got there. I could feel it. People crowded around waiting to be let in. Paparazzi focused on the VIP entrance.

Here we were. This was it.

Songbirds in the Wind. The signs were bright and bold.

Everyone's eyes were fixed on our car as it pulled up outside the VIP entrance, red carpet waiting as the attendants stepped forward to open our doors.

They looked very shocked as I stepped out, and shocked to a whole other level as Lucian stepped out and joined me. Yes. It was us. A Constantine and a Morelli standing together.

And that's when it went crazy. Absolutely fucking crazy. Lights flashing, and cameras clicking and journalists racing forward to get shots of us up close.

Holy Jesus, I was proud. I held Lucian's hand with my chin up high and my smile alight, posing for the press before we began our walk along the red carpet, along with the Quentins.

The press were calling out questions. Someone shoved a microphone right in my face.

"Elaine! Elaine! Were you kidnapped? Give us a statement!"

I gave them a statement. A very simple one,

with a smile. "I wasn't kidnapped, there has been a misunderstanding. I've been with Lucian Morelli and I'm very happy. He's my partner now."

All fear was lost under that pure burst of excitement. All thoughts of our families taking a swipe at us was lost under the bliss as the press went even more crazy with the camera flashes and questions. We ignored the rest of them, just kept on walking.

The red carpet steps lasted a lifetime and a heartbeat both at once. The theater was beautiful when we hit the entrance hall. We were guided to our VIP balcony and the view of the stage was incredible. I took my seat by the railing, leaning forward to check out the full scope of the place. It was everything I'd dreamed it would be.

"And here we are," Lucian whispered to me. "A couple for the world to see. It's an honor, Elaine. A true honor."

"Ditto," I said, with a grin. "Being anywhere with you is an honor, Lucian. I didn't know it was possible to love anyone as much as I love you."

His grin was amazing, nothing like his trademark smirk. "Ditto."

The lights lowered to darkness, bursting to brightness again as the curtains pulled back and the show began. The music was so good. The orchestra was outstanding, and so were the performers on stage.

The story was about two birds separated by the bitter cold and wind, both of them believing the other was dead and not being able to live without them, searching desperately for the other even though they believed they were gone.

I was crying by the end, giving a standing ovation alongside Lucian and the Quentins with my hands in the air.

I only hoped we'd be able to do plenty more of these musicals, because they were magic. Magic.

Lucian knew I was crying with the emotion of the story when he took my hand and led me out onto the landing to make our descent.

"We'll be doing plenty more of this," he assured me, and wiped away my tears with his thumb.

"Thank you," I said.

"There's no thanks to give," he replied. "The pleasure is all mine."

The paparazzi were ready and waiting for us all over again when we left the theater. This time we dashed right past them, taking a dive into the limo before the Quentins slid in and joined us.

Devon let out a breath once we were back in our seats, letting out a guffaw of a laugh.

"Well, we're all still alive. Thumbs-up for that."

Lucian laughed along with him, and he gave him a thumbs-up. An actual thumbs-up, which made me laugh too.

Yeah, these were our friends now. I knew in my heart they always would be.

"Time for the after-party!" Francesca said with a grin, but Lucian shook his head, then smiled at me.

"Not for us. We have somewhere else to go."

I had no idea what he was talking about, but Devon did. "Ah, yes. You'll be taking the limo to Soho. Of course."

I'd heard of Soho as a part of London, but our destination was a mystery to me. Lucian put a finger to my lips as I began to ask questions.

"Wait and see," he told me, and I did as I was told, mind spinning as to where the hell we could be going. He looked…simmering. Intense. Excited in the very darkest of ways. Truly Lucian Morelli.

The limo dropped Devon and Francesca at some grand hotel a short way from the theater.

"See you later." Francesca waved along with

Devon, and we waved back but stayed in the back seat and kept on rolling.

"Tell me where we're going," I pleaded with a grin, but Lucian smirked.

"No," he said. "Wait until you're shown."

The street we pulled into was almost empty. The limo dropped us off outside a set of un-marked doors with two security guards outside, big and gruff. I still had no idea where the hell we were stepping into as the driver let us out onto the sidewalk.

The security guys looked as taken aback as the West End paparazzi had as Lucian led me up to the doors.

"We're expected," he told them. "Your owner, Andy, told me to head right in."

They looked at each other for a long second, then swung open the doors for us without question, letting us walk straight inside.

My eyes were shooting all over the place when they closed the doors behind us. We were standing in a red reception room with a woman with green hair and piercings sitting behind the counter.

She saw us and the recognition was clear all over her face. It took a few seconds for her to compose herself, clearly as surprised by our presence as everyone else we'd crossed paths with that evening.

"Um, hi," she said, struggling for words. "Welcome to Club Explicit."

It was when I saw the couple on the stairs ahead of us that I realized what Club Explicit was, but of course that made sense. Club *Explicit*. It was a dirty one. A BDSM club. I could see it by the crop in a guy's hand as he made his way upstairs alongside a woman in nothing but a thong.

My heart was absolutely pounding when I saw the lust in Lucian's eyes.

He gestured to the stairs. "Let's go check out Club Explicit," he said. "I hope you're ready to show me what an obedient little doll you really are."

Chapter Twenty-Six

Lucian

I'D HEARD EXCELLENT things about Club Explicit. When I was setting up Violent Delights, my own BDSM club back home in NYC, it had been one of the places I'd investigated heavily online in my research. I'd been meaning to visit for quite some time, but I never expected to be doing so with such a delicious creature on my arm. Let alone a woman I was totally in love with.

The mural on the wall as we climbed the stairs was a marvel in itself, but that didn't surprise me. I'd heard that one of London's best street artists had been at work on it. Everything from the lighting and the booths in the main bar, right through to the grand stage and the opulence of the dance floor were testament to the quality and prestige of this venue.

It suited us.

This visit would kick the ass of any damn West End after-party, for sure.

Elaine was her usual wide-eyed self as we headed up to the bar. The girl behind it was a sweet little thing in pigtails, with a lip piercing that gave her a sweet little pout to match. As with everyone else, she stared in shock as we approached, stumbling over her words as she asked what we were drinking. Her shock didn't get any less obvious when I replied.

"Two mineral waters."

She served them up for us with shaking hands, a nervous smile on her pretty little face.

Under previous circumstances, I'd have had her over my knee taking a spanking in a heartbeat, but not anymore. Now it was only Elaine in my world.

We took seats at the bar, looking around the room. It was busy, but not heaving. People were clearly very well acquainted with each other, the atmosphere was tense, but in a magnificent way. I'd never have expected to admit it, but this club was actually better than mine back home in NYC. I'd never have expected to believe *anything* would be better than something of mine, but I had to give credit where it was due. Club Explicit was better than Violent Delights. It kicked its fucking ass.

One thing was for sure, we looked out of place amongst the host of hot-looking freaks in this place. There was nobody else in a tuxedo, and Elaine was shining like a beautiful beacon in her ball gown to the whole damn club. As people began to notice us, heads began to turn en masse, people checking us out with disbelief and a clear rush of excitement. Generally though, they kept their distance. All besides one cocky creature.

The very attractive woman took a seat at the bar next to us, dressed in a black latex catsuit with her jet-black hair swept back into a high ponytail. Her confidence was faultless.

"Hello," she said, with a self-assured smile on her face.

It was Elaine who replied first, with a wave. "Hello."

"I'm Raven," the woman told us, and held out a hand.

My princess shook it with vigor.

"Elaine," she said, and Raven smirked.

"Yes. You are easily recognizable as Elaine," she replied, then turned her attention to me. "And you are also easily recognizable as Lucian. Nice to meet you both."

People didn't usually refer to me on a first name basis in an initial meeting, but with her I didn't seem to mind it. I liked her. I didn't usually like people at first sight, or *ever* in fact, but with her, there was a shine of authenticity. Yes. I liked her. I liked Raven a lot.

I liked her even more when a stunning blonde girl arrived to sit next to her, taking her hand.

"This is my girlfriend, Cara," Raven told us, and the girl waved.

"Hi."

"Hi," Elaine said, and in that one single instant I knew these girls would be her friends. Instinct is a very powerful thing when it strikes.

"Your first time in Club Explicit," Cara commented, stating the very obvious.

I found myself nodding and answering with no sarcasm whatsoever. At odds with my usual self.

"Yes, our first time in Club Explicit."

"Won't be your last," Raven said, with a laugh. "I'm sure you'll have a very good time here."

I found myself nodding at that, too.

"Playrooms are over there," Cara said, pointing to a corridor by the dance floor. "They're great. You'll want to check them out."

But no. I wouldn't.

I knew exactly what I would be checking out. I'd known it from the very instant we'd walked into the bar.

The stage.

I'd be checking out the damn stage.

"Here they come," Raven said, gesturing up to the very stage I was thinking about.

Elaine sat forward on her stool to get a clearer view, and the lights dimmed down on the dance floor, lighting up the stage like the West End theater we'd seen earlier. Incredibly dramatic. Enough to make my pulse race.

I had no idea who *they* were who were coming, but I was very interested to find out.

Elaine asked Raven the question.

"Who's coming up on stage?"

Cara was the one who answered, with a filthy grin on her face. "Masque and Cat. They are Explicit superstars. You'll see why in a minute."

The whole room's attention was up there, which was also an unusual feeling, given that almost everywhere I went in the world, everyone's attention was always on me.

It only took a moment as the figures appeared on stage to realize why.

The woman was beautiful. Beautiful, naked

and proud of it, her dark hair cascading down her back as she raised her hands for the shackles coming down from the ceiling. But it wasn't just her who was grabbing the attention, it was the hulk of a man who appeared behind her.

He was absolutely fucking huge. Huge, toned, and quite possibly the most confident guy I'd ever seen outside of myself. He reeked of it. Pure, unabashed confidence, without a hint of arrogance. He was in a leather mask that covered half of his face, and that made him look all the more intimidating. That combined with the fact that he had a huge dark tattoo on his chest. A two-headed dragon creature, its tail curling around his back.

"Wow," Elaine said, and Raven nodded.

She leaned over close enough to nudge my princess with a smirk on her face. "I did that tattoo for him. The chimera."

"You're a tattoo artist?"

"Yes," she said. "I am."

Again I had another flash of instinct. A very definite one.

My princess was going to get tattooed by her, and I was going to be the one choosing the marks she'd be wearing forever more.

Conversation sure as fuck dried up when the big guy grabbed his flogger and started trailing it down his submissive's spine. She tipped her head back, ready and hungry. A true submissive. That much was very obvious.

Fuck, how he hurt her.

Fuck, how she wanted it.

Whimpering turned to squeals, and squeals turned to gasps, and gasps turned to tears.

Tears turned to begging for more.

The flogger turned to a crop, and a crop turned to a cane, and that beast of a man took that woman like a serious fucking master. I felt strangely competitive as I watched him. I also felt strangely competitive as I watched the way my little doll was watching him hurting his woman, transfixed. I was jealous.

He was the first damn man I'd been jealous of in my whole fucking life, but again it was bizarre, because I didn't feel any malice in it. Nothing but an insane sense of...respect. I didn't give respect very easily.

The master slapped his girl's pussy until she was clamping her thighs closed tight and then, when she was trembling and quaking, he barked at her to spread them wide.

She did just as she was told. Good little doll.

Even I was surprised when he fisted her. Hard. Right up there on stage, in the spotlight, in front of the whole damn room. Jesus Christ, she took it like a perfect whore, working herself onto his fist, even though she was gasping with the pain.

My cock was hard watching them, but it wasn't hard for them. It was hard for the girl at my side, picturing her up there in the same fucking shackles, bracing herself to take the pain.

I looked across at her, my Elaine, and she was still transfixed. I saw the way she was clenching her own thighs together under her gown and could imagine how her heart was fluttering.

She liked it. She wanted it.

My little doll wanted to be taken in shackles, just as I wanted to take her that way.

That sealed her fate. My beautiful princess had sealed her fate.

The man they called Masque took his woman until she was a quivering wreck, then fucked her ass as she moaned, still strung up tight as the club watched them in awe. It put the West End musical to shame.

Raven was nodding at us with a clear *yeah, told you so* when the lights came back up and the couple left the stage to thunderous applause. Even my princess was clapping and whooping.

"Explicit superstars," Raven reiterated. "Nobody ever gets enough of them."

I most definitely wasn't expecting it when the two of them headed right over toward us, the girl still teetering on wobbly legs as she reached Raven and pulled her in for a hug.

Masque was an even bigger beast up close. He checked us out, both me and Elaine, and gave a smile.

"Welcome to Club Explicit."

He held out a hand and I took it, well aware it was covered in his pretty submissive's juices.

"Lucian," I said, only registering that I'd introduced myself on first name terms after the word had left my mouth.

"James," he replied, and Raven let out a laugh.

"My God, Masque, did you just tell him your actual name?" She leaned closer to me. "You must be damn royalty for James to call himself James."

I guess we were damn royalty though, and we always would be.

"Have you checked out the playrooms?" James asked me, but I shook my head.

"No," I told him. "I have more pressing interests."

He read my mind and smirked at me.

"You'll have the whole place lifting the roof if you give them a second show tonight."

Elaine's eyes widened like saucers at that, pretty little mouth dropping open.

"On stage?" she asked, attention all on me. "We might be going up on stage?!"

I got straight up to my feet, cock throbbing hard enough in my pants that it hurt.

"No might about it, baby," I told her. "Get your sweet little pussy over there right fucking now."

CHAPTER TWENTY-SEVEN

Elaine

EVERYBODY'S EYES WERE fixed on me as I made my way across the room, heading up to the stage. I'd never felt so exposed in my life, and I wasn't even naked, my ball gown was still glittering bright, sweeping around my feet with every step.

Lucian led the way up the stairs at the side of the stage, then presented me under the spotlights, showing me off to the gathering crowd with that beautiful pride on his face, and I felt it. Even under the tension, and the nerves, and the fear, he was the core of me. My heart and my soul.

With the lights blinding me from up above, people were largely shadows, but I could still see them gathering closer, their eyes on me.

I'd never have imagined myself in this position, up on stage in a BDSM club, about to be fucked and hurt in front of a crowd by the ultimate lord of my life, Lucian Morelli. The craziness of this situation put the red carpet walk to shame. I was shivering, goose prickled, pulse racing in fight or flight.

I knew I would never be fleeing from my monster. I knew I would do whatever he commanded me to do, and I wanted that. I *needed* that.

I was still flushed from watching the couple up on stage before us, still excited, because from the very first moment I'd seen them up there, I'd wanted to be that woman up on stage, held firm in the shackles.

Only I hadn't wanted it to be her beast of a man up there alongside me.

I'd wanted it to be *my* monster.

His hands were firm and steady as he took hold of the shackles above me and bound my hands in the cuffs. I let out a gasp as he pulled them high, stretching my arms up tight above me, high enough that I was on tiptoes, even in my heels.

His body was so hot as he pressed himself tight to my back, even through his tuxedo. His voice was a gravelly whisper in my ear.

"You'll take what you're given, Elaine, and it's

going to hurt."

A whole new wave of shivers raced through me, and I was back there in front of him in my mind, right from the very beginning, when I'd known he'd give me pain and I'd wanted it so much I was begging him.

I closed my eyes when he pulled my dress loose and let it drop to the floor around my feet, my heart racing all the more at the cheer from the crowd. And there I was, teetering in front of the watching audience in just my heels and panties. My panties which were already wet from how much I wanted this.

I knew my cut was still clear on my ribs, but it was already beginning to heal. To fade. To become irrelevant. Enough that the crowd in front of me didn't freak out at me under the lights.

"Step," Lucian said, and I raised my feet one at a time as he pulled my dress out from underneath me.

Then he moved away.

It felt like I was there for an age, standing bare for the spectators.

I heard him behind me, clearly swishing implements from a rack. It was a flogger he presented me with first, only he didn't run it down my back like the beast before him had teased his woman. Lucian curled it right around my tits from the very first swing, catching a nipple so hard it made me jump in the chains, and that's when it truly took me, the craving for the hurt running right through my veins like a calling.

I was ready for it when he did it again, only this time I didn't jump, I moaned, bracing myself proud.

He tugged my panties down my thighs.

"Step," he said again, and I was ready, stepping out of the lace.

I was naked apart from my heels, nipples hard and still stinging. He reached his hands around from behind me, sliding them across my skin to twist and pull to turn that stinging to a hard, strong pain.

"Take it," he said, and I tipped my head back against his shoulder, offering my tits to his hands and he twisted and pulled some more. His breath was on my neck and I found I was smiling, eyes still closed as I focused on his touch and nothing more.

His fingers slid down my ribs, tickling, but again he was so careful not to hurt the pain he didn't cause. I clenched my stomach muscles as they swept their way further down.

"Spread yourself for me," he whispered. "Be a good girl and spread your thighs as far as they'll fucking go."

I was a good girl for him. I spread my thighs as far as they would fucking go, putting all of my weight on those shackles.

His fingers spread my pussy lips, exposing my clit to the crowd. I gasped as he circled the right spot, teasing me just enough that I let out a moan as he pushed three fingers inside me in one thrust.

"Show them what a horny little doll you are," he ordered me. "Squirm on my fingers."

I did.

I squirmed on his fingers, even though he was so brutal it hurt.

When he yanked those fingers from me, his breaths were faster. I could feel the swell in his pants against my ass and he was so hard that it made me alive with a new sense of pride. I wanted the crowd to see me be good enough to please him. I wanted them to see I could drive a man like Lucian Morelli crazy because he wanted me so much. Not any of the other stunning women in this room who were more experienced than I was, but *me*. Only me.

"Suck me clean," he said and pushed his wet fingers into my mouth and I sucked him so hard I was slurping.

"Good girl," he said, and then he became my true monster. My monster for the world around us to see.

His hands slapped and twisted, setting my skin alive. My pussy was so sore after he spanked it long and hard that I tried to close my thighs, but he barked that I wasn't to fucking disobey him.

The flogger was a gem, trailing, then stinging, everywhere from my back, to my ass, and my tits, everywhere desperate for more…but he was as careful a tiger as ever, playing just the right places of me in just the right ways.

The crop attacked my thighs with perfect precision, making me cry out a little every time it landed by my pussy, so tender. His fingers fucked me between rounds of thwacks and I moaned for him, giving him my insides like a whore craving more.

My mouth was already open, panting when he kissed me, and that's when I realized it. My eyes were still closed. My eyes had been closed the whole time he was using me.

Turns out, he'd realized it before I had.

"Look at me," he commanded, and I opened them to find him standing right there, his face beautiful enough that I sucked in a breath. The dirty glint in his stare, hungry for me. His stunning mouth that made mine water, needing his spit and his tongue more than I'd ever needed champagne.

"Suck," he said, again reading my mind, and I sucked his tongue as he kissed me like a kid needing a lollipop, still so firm in the shackles that I moaned for more when he pulled away and I couldn't reach him.

He stepped away and my open eyes landed on the room. On the figures there staring up at me. At the gathered crowd, some of them so close that I could see their faces under the glare of the spotlights. Every single one of them was looking at me like I was a queen.

Yes.

I wanted this.

It was a mirror to everything I'd hated in my past. People playing with me when I didn't want them to, looking at me like a dirty little piece of shit who meant nothing.

This was a whole other world. Lucian Morelli playing with me when I wanted nothing more than his touch and his commands, while the whole room stared at me like I was a goddess who meant *everything*.

I was so happy when Lucian stepped back up beside me with a smirk and placed a cane against my tits. I nodded, smiling right back, my stare all on him.

He caned my tits so hard I was crying out, but still I was offering myself for more, desperate for the stripes, for the pain, for the marks on my skin.

His marks on my skin.

I was trembling as he caned my thighs, striping me up all over again.

He caned me until I was panting and struggling to take it, even in my submissive state. Then he played with my clit, his fingers a perfect tease. He caned my ass until I was crying out, broken, and then his fingers played me some more, over and over and over, until I was in a blur in the most blissful of ways.

Still that room stared up at me, transfixed.

I didn't know it was coming when he lowered my shackles and dropped me down to my knees. The chains were hanging loose when he presented himself in front of me, his pants unbuckled and his cock hard enough that it was dark with desperation.

Oh, how he fucked my mouth. I gagged and retched and spluttered, dribbling spit down onto the floor. He took hold of my throat and choked me as I tried to suck him, my eyes watering as I stared up at his face. I was moaning as he stole his cock from me, moaning harder as he got down onto his knees behind me and rubbed himself against my slit.

Oh, how he fucked my pussy. Oh, how I moaned, chains rattling and the crowd cheering as I slammed myself back onto his cock with every thrust.

He took my hair, twisted and pulled, showing me off as I moaned, angling himself just right so I bucked and gasped and came for him.

And then he came for me.

Lucian Morelli came for me in front of a crowded room, grunting as he spurted inside me.

I'd never been so proud in my life.

I was his woman. His whore. His doll.

I was the love of his life.

God, it was bliss. Pure, absolute bliss. I was grinning when he unbuckled the shackles and helped me to my feet in the most gracious of ways, smiling back at me in the most gorgeous way I'd ever seen him smile.

He helped me back into my dress with gentle hands, and I knew full well I was marked all over by his brutality. I was buzzing from it so brightly that it felt like a crime to cover it back up with the fabric.

The crowd had already begun dispersing when we climbed down from the stage and made our way back over to the bar. I must have been glowing like a beacon, flinching as I sat down on a stool next to the woman who'd introduced herself as Raven.

She laughed at me, a lovely genuine giggle that was almost like a cackle.

"Told you it won't be your last time here," she said, and I laughed along with her.

She was damn right on that.

We were in there for a long, long time, chatting away quite happily to Raven, and her girlfriend, and James and Cat. They were amazing, treating us like any other clubgoer and not as people in the media glare all over the world. I loved it. All of it.

It was almost morning when we finally got into a cab, all set to head back to Quentin Manor and a nice, warm bed. Lucian was only glancing at his cell when he pulled a face. I was close enough to see the twenty-five missed calls, all with the same number.

A number from over in the US.

Lucian recognized it though. I could see it from his scowl.

He didn't even get a chance to talk about it before his cell started up all over again. It was still on silent from the club, but the screen was flashing, showing it was still that same number.

He answered with a "what?" and I heard the voice at the other end, my head still on Lucian's shoulder, close enough to hear.

The voice was seething. Nasty.

"You've gone way too fucking far this time, Son. It's time to say goodbye."

Lucian was right back at him, his tone nasty to match.

"Don't start a war," he said. "It won't be a pretty one."

And then he hung up the call.

CHAPTER TWENTY-EIGHT

Lucian

I'D KNOWN THE war was coming, and I knew my family would be out for the attack, just as Elaine's would be. Still, it didn't stop the shiver up my spine as I realized afresh what would be headed our way. At least one attempt on our lives.

I'd been busy in the background, preparing security. I was ready to fight right back, standing up for our place in the world.

We could do this. *I* could do this.

Elaine looked scared as I turned in the back seat to face her. She was biting her lip, terrified.

"They are going to come after us, aren't they?" she asked.

"Yes," I replied. "They are, but they aren't going to win, sweetheart. I can promise you that. This is our world now. *Ours.*"

She nodded, even if there was still that bubble

of fear in her below the surface. Fuck, how I wanted her. I wanted to be her blanket of protection and her lord of hope, with every single step we could take.

The cab driver barely said a word as we pulled up back at Quentin Manor. Elaine winced as I helped her out of the back seat, tenderness taking hold of her. Fuck, I'd hit her nice and hard.

I paid the driver and he sped away, leaving us to ascend the manor steps as the sky showed the first taste of dawn all around us. Hell, it was a late one.

Elaine acknowledged my thoughts, matching just right with hers. "Wow, it's late. I'm so tired."

I smirked as I opened the main door for her.

"Yes, baby. It's very late and you must be very tired."

She was grinning an innocent grin as we began to climb the stairs up to our wing.

"You going to snuggle me tight in bed, then?" she asked.

"Get your sweet ass up there and find out," I pushed, and she did. She sashayed that sweet ass up there with a spring in her step despite her body undoubtedly aching from my blows.

We showered together, slowly. I soaped her nice and gently, but she was still flinching as she smiled. Her skin was a masterpiece, already darkening, brewing with bruises. She was delicious, but now wasn't the time to feast on her.

We did snuggle up in bed together and she fell asleep within a few short minutes of me stroking her hair. It took me a lot longer to close my eyes, staring at the light of the morning glowing through the drapes.

My mind was full of the plans I'd made. The purchases I'd made. The declarations I was ready to make.

My father could lash out from overseas if he thought I was unprepared for that. Elaine's family would be brewing on their own ideas to the same tune, but they could get fucked too. We had too much of a network of power over here already, and that was growing every minute.

The Quentins didn't organize breakfast for us, undoubtedly well aware that we would have had an exceptionally late night. I rolled over after a fitful slumber and Elaine was still sleeping peacefully, oblivious to the world.

I watched her, replaying the vision of her in shackles over and over. We'd certainly be repeating that experience, but first I had more pressing engagements.

Devon was outside playing tennis on the

manor court. I saw him through the window as I dressed myself quietly, leaving my princess sleeping as I headed out. He smiled when I came into view, waving his *later* wave to his assistant playing along with him. He dropped his racket against the fence as he joined me, still catching his breath.

"So how was Club Explicit?" he asked, and I smiled back.

"Just as I'd hoped. Excellent."

He nodded. "Good. I'm glad London is living up to your expectations."

Yes, it was. It was surpassing even the wildest hopes I'd been holding onto as Elaine and I had boarded that plane with fake IDs.

It was Devon who raised the subject I'd been planning to question. He leaned in closer, even though there was nobody even vaguely close enough to hear us.

"The timescale is on schedule," he told me. "They will be here before nightfall. The outbuilding at the bottom of the far paddock."

"Thank you," I said and that villain in me was alive and burning through me.

"Dinner this evening?" he asked, and I nodded.

"It would be a pleasure."

"A pleasure for us, too. Roast beef with all the trimmings."

"Sounds delicious," I acknowledged, and we made our way back to the house.

Francesca was waiting for him in the sitting room, clearly wanting his attention, so I made my exit, heading back upstairs to the wing that was beginning to feel like our own. Still, that would be coming to an end soon enough. We would soon have a manor all of our own.

Elaine was up and getting dressed as I walked in, still flinching as she pulled her jeans up over her bruised thighs.

"Ouch," she said, with a smirk. "I'll be feeling this for days."

I loved that. My eyes must have said it all because her cheeks reddened, her smirk turning to an innocent smile, eating up my happiness. The thrum of the night before was still magic between us.

"Are we eating with the Quentins this evening?" she asked, and I nodded.

"Roast beef with all the trimmings, apparently."

"Sounds nice."

Conversation was brimming heavy with that need for each other, but today it wasn't about sex, or pain, or consuming flesh. This was about the closeness. The need for connection.

We lay there together for a long afternoon, watching crappy TV and munching on snacks delivered from the kitchen as we carried on the random question chatter, only this time it was interspersed with snippets of memories and funny stories that had us both laughing.

We were still laughing as dinnertime reached us and we headed down to the dining room, taking our places opposite Devon and Francesca at the table.

Throughout the meal the women were talking nonstop about the West End and the red carpet and the musical, but there was a secret nod between Devon and me across the table as soon as his cell buzzed with a ping. He excused us for some business conversation after dessert, leaving the ladies chatting about the next series of musicals due for the West End.

I knew exactly where we were going. I walked alongside Devon Quentin without a word, following his march through the manor grounds to the paddock at the bottom of the pasture.

The outbuilding was there, standing tall.

"I'll leave you here," he said, and slapped a hand between my shoulders. "Everything you asked for has been delivered. Nobody is close enough to hear a thing."

I tipped my head. "Much appreciated."

"I'll make sure the women enjoy their evening, I'm sure they will be very distracted," he assured me.

I had no doubt about that.

Devon left me standing there in the twilight. I flexed my knuckles before I stepped up to the main barn entrance, swinging the big wooden door wide open to step inside.

There were two figures hanging from a whole set of shackles of their own, only this time there were no spotlights like in Club Explicit, just some orange glowing lanterns to allow me to see. There was no crowd cheering for the hurt, just two sick fucks begging that I didn't kill them. Begging that there had been a misunderstanding and they had never crossed the Morellis.

It gave me a huge rush of pleasure to tell Baron Rawlings and Lord Eddington that it wasn't the Morellis I was taking retribution for. It gave me an even larger rush of pleasure to tell them exactly who I was claiming retribution for and why.

Elaine Constantine, because I loved her. Because I adored her. Because she was the woman of my dreams and heart and whole fucking soul.

I showed them how much I loved her with every slash of the blade. I paid them back for every time they'd taken sick pleasure from the woman I loved by taking sick pleasure of my own from hurting them.

They'd been begging for their lives when I'd first stepped in to join them. They were begging for their deaths when I finally pulled my cell out of my pocket and told them to confess their sins on camera.

They confessed their sins. They gave me the details of the fellowship on-screen and how they'd been a part of it and just what the fuck they'd done. There was a truth in their eyes and voices that could never be disputed. Their memories matching and perfect. Memories of themselves, and Reverend Lynch, and the other fools still on my list to be wiped out for ever.

Plus memories of the sicko at the center of Elaine's fate—Lionel Constantine and how he'd delivered her for her abuse when she was nothing more than a gentle little girl looking for acceptance and love.

It was well into the night when I finally stepped back out from the barn, my shirt red and slick, leaving two corpses behind me, still in chains. My hands were tainted scarlet, blood crusted under my fingernails.

There was only Devon in the sitting room when I arrived back into the manor. He gave me a nod and pressed a button on his cell phone, no doubt to alert the cleanup team.

I said two simple words that were straight from my cold black heart.

"Thank you."

"You need a cleanup team of your own," he laughed, gesturing at my outfit.

"I'm sure Elaine will help me out on that front," I laughed back. "And on that note."

"I'll see you in the morning," he said. "Six a.m. start?"

"I'll be ready," I told him, and I would be. I'd be preened and polished and ready to begin a whole new week of deals and planning and negotiations. Both business and pleasure. Pleasure of the greatest kind on earth.

Elaine was watching another round of crappy TV when I walked through the bedroom door. Her eyes shot straight over to me, and her mouth dropped open as she scrabbled to her feet, dashing over to run her hands up and down my bloodied chest, checking me over.

"Not mine," I reassured her and took hold of

her hands to kiss her knuckles.

"Then whose?" she asked. "What the hell happened?!"

I told her. Slowly.

I watched her soak in the details, breaths hitching with an obvious combination of relief and gratitude that I'd destroyed the evil cunts for her. She cried pretty, moving tears that almost choked me up to match.

We took a shower when I finished recounting the events and she soaped me down, scrubbing me with delicate fingers, watching the blood swirl away down the drain.

Then it was her turn to say the two simple words, straight from her heart. Only her heart wasn't cold and black. Hers was warm and loving. Beautiful like the rest of her as her eyes pooled with a fresh round of tears.

"Thank you."

"I don't deserve a thank you," I told her. "The pleasure was mine."

I meant it. I'd do whatever it took to make my princess happy in life. I'd love and protect and serve. I'd hurt, and barter, and bribe. I'd raise her on a pedestal for the whole world to see, and savor every heartbeat of her in my arms.

And I'd show her that.

I'd show her that in no uncertain terms very soon, in a whole different way than killing two of the pieces of shit who emotionally killed her.

I'd show her right at the top of the London Eye, right where she belonged.

CHAPTER TWENTY-NINE

Elaine

I HAD NO idea where we were going in the limo but life was buzzing around us as we headed into London from Quentin Manor. They weren't with us, Devon and Francesca. This wasn't one of the premieres we'd been talking about, and this wasn't a late-night visit to Club Explicit that Lucian and I had been planning. This was something else. Something that had Lucian in a new tailored tuxedo and me in the little black dress I'd picked out so happily with Francesca.

There were security vehicles surrounding the limo as we drove into the city, keeping our safety their priority. So far there had been no sign of attack from either my family or Lucian's, and it was seeming to be less likely—security growing stronger and associates promising even greater protection.

Maybe, just maybe, we'd be safe in our new future. I was daring to believe it.

I shot forward in my seat when the pods of the London Eye appeared in view, and my heart leapt as I pressed my face to the window, because I knew it right there and then. I knew just where we were headed.

"Really?" I asked Lucian with a squeal. "We're going to the London Eye?"

God, his smirk. "Wait and see."

I couldn't sit still. I just couldn't. I was squirming back and forth, my attention zipping from him to the window and back again on constant loop, still flying high with the excitement.

Oh my God, we were going to do it. We were going to ride the London Eye as the sun set, lighting up the river Thames in perfection. It would be *perfection*!

"Thank you, thank you, thank you!" I gushed at Lucian as the limo pulled up at the entrance, next to the line barriers.

Except there were no line barriers. Not tonight. There was only a red carpet, lined with security guards and attendants.

They helped me from the limo and I stared up at the Eye with a lump in my throat as Lucian took my side. It was really happening. It would be a dream come true.

There wasn't a single person around. Nobody in the line. Nobody in the pods. Not a single sign of life as Lucian guided me along the carpet, all the way up to a waiting pod.

He stepped aside, giving me a little bow as I walked in, and there I was, spinning around with that lump still in my throat, trying to comprehend the reality of truly being in this space. My dream.

Being in this space *with* my dream.

I let out a squeal as the pod started moving and we began the ascent, just the two of us holding each other tight, mineral waters in our hands, staring out at the incredible view.

"Thank you so much," I said again, and the lump in my throat showed itself with the dip of my voice.

"You are more than welcome, princess," he told me. "You are my life, this is just one tiny little testament to that."

We pointed out landmarks with smiles, everything etching itself into my memory forever. The Shard. Westminster. The Tower of London.

I still couldn't believe it. Lucian had taken over the whole of the London Eye, all for me.

It was when we reached the very top, and the very height of our spin, that Lucian let me go from his arms. I turned to face him, shocked at his body moving away from mine, but not as shocked as I felt when he dropped down in front of me onto his knees. Only it wasn't onto his *knees*.

It was on one knee. One.

Lucian Morelli was on one knee in front of me, at the very top of the London Eye.

It was then when the fireworks lit up the Thames in front of us. Bursts of pure sparks flying high into the sunset and glistening diamonds on the water. I was blown away by the crazy emotion of it, because surely not…surely it couldn't be…

But it was. It was.

"Will you marry me, Elaine Constantine?" Lucian asked me, and presented the ring. A full-on glittering diamond in a little black box.

I couldn't speak. I didn't have a voice. Didn't have a breath. Didn't have anything but a nod as the tears fell. The lump in my throat had nothing on the gushes of happy tears that ran down my cheeks as Lucian got back up to his feet and slipped my engagement ring onto my ring finger.

He held me tight and kissed me deep, then turned us both back to face the fireworks still bursting all around us. Only my eyes weren't on the fireworks, they couldn't be. They were too transfixed on the diamond on my finger.

I was going to marry Lucian Morelli.

Holy fuck, I was engaged to Lucian Morelli.

He held me tight as the pod descended back to the ground. It was slow and perfect, the atmosphere between us so loved up that my heart could have burst for real.

The attendants were ready and waiting for us when our descent reached its end, helping us back onto solid ground with smiles and congratulations.

The red carpet felt so long and incredible as we made our way back to the street. There were paparazzi gathered, managing to capture just a few pictures of us walking together before the security guards ushered them away.

"They were given minimum access, don't worry," Lucian told me. "Believe me, baby, I've got so much security around us they could fight a war."

"Amazing," I said, because it was. It was amazing. Us being *alive* was amazing, after betraying both families and their vendettas back home across the Atlantic.

He had his usual smirk on his face as we approached the waiting limo. "It'll be even more amazing when you see the Morelli-Constantine Manor by High Wycombe. The security is so well ingrained you won't even see their presence, but believe me, princess, they will be there. People won't be able to step within a quarter mile of the place without being wiped out for their intrusion."

"We have a manor?"

My pulse couldn't race any faster. The surprises were piled too high. My heart soaring too fast.

"Yes," Lucian said. "We have a manor. Just you wait and see."

"When?!" I asked him. "When will I see it?"

An attendant opened the limo door and I slipped into the back seat ahead of Lucian. They shut us inside with a smile and wave.

"Now," he told me. "You'll see it now. We're heading right on over. Francesca and Devon are already waiting there to celebrate."

My hands were shaking as I checked out my ring finger for the thousandth time already.

The limo pulled away and the security cars drove along with us until we were out of the city, well on our way to the new manor in the darkness.

I couldn't wait.

Holy hell, I couldn't wait. We were going home. Home.

Home to a whole new home of our own.

The signs on the road started showing High Wycombe getting closer.

It was only when the distance seemed to be getting further away rather than closer that Lucian leaned forward in the seat and cast a scowl at the driver.

"The sooner the fucking better, please," he said. "Get your act together."

But that's when the interior locks sounded out loud around us and the screen between us and the driver closed up tight.

"What the fuck—" Lucian began, but then he shifted again, staring at the driver through the glass, and I saw him realize something. Saw something slam him like a hammerblow.

His eyes were wild when he turned back to face me, grabbing me by the hand before trying the doors, but they were locked up tight.

"What's happening?!" I asked him. "Lucian?! What the hell?!"

I'd never seen him scared before.

I'd never seen him frantic like he was when he tried to elbow the window until it smashed, but still he couldn't break it.

It only took one sight of the driver staring back at me in the rearview mirror before I knew exactly what was happening.

It wasn't the same driver as the one who'd taken us to the Eye. It wasn't any one of the drivers who'd been responsible for driving us around since we first stepped foot on their soil.

I cried out as the limo pulled off the road at a random junction marked with a sign that said "Briar Dene Village, *please drive slowly.*" But we didn't drive slowly. The limo sped through the village and I cried out harder as it screeched and rumbled up onto a gravel path, heading off road into some woodland, lined high with trees. I was so scared. So fucking scared I couldn't breathe as we came to a stop.

Lucian's hand was tight in mine when the driver got out of the front seat and came for us. The gun was already aimed at us as he opened the door and ordered us out.

Lucian moved first, keeping me firmly behind him.

"Whatever they've offered you for doing this…" he said, but the guy shook his head.

"Don't even think about trying to buy me," he replied. "I've been pro Morelli my whole life, you ain't got shit to hold over me. Now, get out of the car slowly. I know you're packing. Hand it over. Try anything and I'll blow your bitch's brains out."

Lucian did as he was told, revealing the holster beneath his jacket, carefully taking the gun from it.

The driver snatched it from him, told us to get to the trunk.

Lucian kept me close behind him as we did as we were told, shuffling to the back of the limo while the driver kept the gun aimed at Lucian. He opened the trunk and there was the original driver, curled up, dead.

"I have orders," the driver said. "And I'm going to be following them. Hurry up."

He took out a cell phone and pointed it at us, and the light came on as he set the video camera rolling.

Once again he gestured us forward, guiding us into a space on the grass.

"Get the fuck over there," he said to Lucian, and Lucian held his hands up as he stepped away from me.

"Stay where you are, Elaine," he said as I made a move to follow him.

"No!" I cried out.

"Stay there, Elaine. This is between me and my fucking father."

The driver laughed. "Not quite. It wasn't actually your father who ordered the hit. It was Elliot fucking Morelli, your own cousin, who wants to take over the company."

"Any last words?" the driver asked Lucian, stepping up closer to get a decent view on camera.

"Yes," Lucian told him, stepping forward so his stomach was pressed to the gun. He looked straight at the cell and pulled a smirk. An evil one. "Go fuck yourself."

I screamed as the gun sounded. Lucian collapsed onto the grass. I rushed over but I didn't get very far, the driver stepping between me and my love before I could reach him.

I was wailing inconsolable, on my knees on the grass when the driver pointed both the cell and the gun at me. "It was all about money," he said. "That's all anyone cares about, whether you're rich or poor. And I'm going to be one of the rich ones, now."

The evening was dark around us, but not so dark that I didn't see the movement of Lucian's body between the driver's legs. It didn't make any sense, because if Lucian wasn't dead, he would be screaming and flopping. He wouldn't be able to hold himself still.

But of course.

He wouldn't.

He wouldn't be feeling a thing. He *couldn't* feel a thing.

I gulped in a breath when my love got to his feet without a sound.

I'll never forget the sound of that knife going in. The driver fell to his knees, dropped the cell and almost dropped the gun. He tried to swing it round but Lucian had him, snatching the gun in a beat.

My love won the battle and fired the next shot.

The driver fell to the ground, bleeding out and wailing before Lucian shot him in the back of the skull, just like the driver should have had the sense to do to him.

Then my perfect lover collapsed.

He collapsed to the ground with his arm clenched to his wound, blood spilling from his mouth as he struggled. "It shouldn't hurt," he murmured to me, looking dazed. "But it does."

I don't know how I had the breath or the voice to make the call to the emergency services from Lucian's cell, pulled out from his tux pocket, but I did it.

"Please hurry," I said to the dispatcher.

I sat next to my fiancé and begged the heavens to save him. Please, please just save him.

My hand was pressed tight to Lucian's bleeding stomach when the sirens and lights showed up, begging them for help as they fought for his life.

Thank fuck, and thank the lord, they managed to get Lucian's breathing steady before we pulled up at the hospital, screeching to a halt outside the emergency entrance.

I waited for him through a long night.

Francesca rushed in to give me a hug and hold me tight. I waited until the morning next to the people who'd become our friends, grateful for the true support I felt from them with every breath.

And then, finally, when the sun was bright outside and London was stirring to life for another day, the doctor arrived to tell me Lucian Morelli was done with surgery, and that he too was stirring with life for another day.

Lucian Morelli was going to make it.

My fiancé was going to survive.

This wasn't a tragedy, after all. It wasn't a love story the way the world understood them. He was my monster, and I was his doll, and we would live together forever.

EPILOGUE

Lucian, one year later

IT'S A BEAUTIFUL thing, having such ultimate power over somebody so powerful. Enough evidence to destroy them if they so much as step a threatening foot onto your turf.

My father accepted my engagement to Elaine Constantine, realizing it wasn't worth the risk or the fight. Elaine and I had enjoyed our engagement very happily in our Morelli-Constantine manor in Bishop's Landing.

I was surprisingly nervous as the day began, waking up alone in bed with a strange rush of flutters in my stomach, still scarred after all these months from taking the bullet. Leo, Tiernan, and Carter were downstairs in the breakfast room, still looking groggy from my bachelor party as they guzzled down black coffee. Devon was telling them about his insurance empire when I joined them. All three of them let out a mocking cheer as I sat myself down at the breakfast table, giving them a smirk that matched my mood. A happy one.

"Here comes the groom," Carter said, reaching over to punch me in the arm. "Never thought I'd see you getting hitched. Never thought it would be to a Constantine."

"There must be something in the water," Leo said, his voice dry. Over the past year I'd learned that he'd fallen for his own Constantine. She'd attend the wedding with him.

"Elaine is worth it," I said, my voice sober.

Devon nodded. "My wife absolutely adores her. Has since the moment they met."

We still had a few hours before the ceremony. The guys started on the whisky as soon as we were dressed up ready for the service. Tiernan was more gruff than the other brothers, but even he had shown up to support me. It touched me more than I thought it would.

We got ready together, a photographer there to document the occasion. Surreal as fuck.

The caterers and wedding planners had already been at work on the manor for days. It looked even more incredibly grand than I'd expected as we set off in the limo for the church, and it should. I'd invested the very best into the very best celebration life could offer.

The church only had a few guests in their seats when the four of us arrived and made our way inside. My brothers took their positions at the entrance, ushers standing proud, and I gave them a thankful nod as I left them to their duties.

It was Devon I'd chosen to be my best man, his place feeling very natural at my side as we stepped into the front pew. My brothers were there next to him, and my sisters in the pews.

"I'm weirdly fucking nervous," I confessed to Devon, and he laughed.

"Never thought I'd see you nervous, Lucian. It's a damn novelty."

The nerves only heightened as the benches filled up with associates, as well as some of my old business acquaintances who'd flown in.

My family sat in the front rows of the groom's side. My mother, looking severe with her begrudging approval of my bride.

Bryant Morelli had been cleared of the worst of it when it was revealed that Elliot had master-minded the plot to kill us. We were a bloodthirsty family, when it came down to it, but I was actually glad that my father hadn't done it. It hadn't been the worst betrayal.

Now the company was mine, and he was only a figurehead over the family.

Elaine's friends were filling up her side of the aisle just as mine were filling up mine. I recognized many of them from local events she'd been attending, all of them giving me a wave as they saw me standing there.

Yes, the room was most certainly filling up.

It was almost full when I saw them. Elaine's sisters. Vivian and Tinsley, looking spectacular in pastel gowns. My heart lurched, thumping like a fucking train, hardly daring to believe they'd shown up for the sister who'd seemingly betrayed their family name. My heart thumped even harder when I saw Harriet, her cousin, stepping in to join them. The cousin that Elaine had cried about missing when we were in London, desperate to see again.

And there was Winston Constantine, along with his new bride. The patriarch of the Constantine family, came to show his support of the union.

Still, my thumping heart had nothing on the fucking speed it thumped when Caroline Constantine, Elaine's mother, came into view and took a seat alongside them. My eyes met hers, staring hard in disbelief. Total, utter disbelief.

I expected nothing but hatred on her face as she stared at me, but it wasn't there. There was nothing but...grace. Grace and...thanks, and holy fuck I felt it. Jesus Christ above, she offered her imperial approval with a small nod of her head.

I'd have stepped right on over to begin dialogue with her if the harpist hadn't started up the beautiful music for the bride's entry. My whole body heated up in the most incredible of ways as I strained to get sight of the church entrance, because even now, after months of imagining it, I couldn't quite believe it. I couldn't believe my love, Elaine, was walking up the aisle.

She'd taken my breath away countless times since the very first moment I'd laid eyes on her, all the way back at Tinsley's ball, but my breath was ripped right from my chest as I saw her there, nervous, her blonde curls swept up behind her, and her white veil positioned so perfectly underneath her tiara. White, because she was pure. Regardless of the sex. Regardless of her history. She was pure in every way that counted.

Her dress was the most intensely beautiful thing I'd ever seen on her. It framed her figure in such a way that would burn itself into my heart forever, flowing around her feet in the most divine of ways with every step.

Elaine was walking up the aisle. To me. My love was walking up the aisle.

Every step was getting closer.

Every step had my whole soul desperate, insane.

It was the guy who utterly despised me that was standing next to her with his arm in hers, all set to give her away. The best friend she'd known since she was a teenager, who I'd knocked out cold when I was hunting her down a year ago. Not exactly the best of introductions to your future wife's bestie, but it was what it was.

As it turned out, Tristan wasn't glaring at me when he delivered her to my side. He managed a smile, and I managed the briefest of smiles back. Her bridesmaids, Francesca, Raven and Cara were grinning bright as they took their seats, but I barely saw them. My eyes were fixed all on Elaine. She was shaking like a leaf as she joined me at the head of the aisle, her beautiful blue eyes, pools of perfect love.

"I have no words," I whispered to her. "None that could do you justice right now."

That's when her innocent smile lit up her face even brighter. "Ditto," she said.

Elaine was so focused on me that she had

barely cast a glance around the guests before the service started. The ceremony started right up, every word etched into the fabric of time, vows of declaration that people had lived by and loved by, for hundreds of years before us.

I took Elaine to be my lawfully wedded wife with a lump in my throat because it meant so much to me.

She took me to be her lawfully wedded husband with a lump in her throat to match, eyes welling up because it meant so much to her.

Devon handed me the rings when they were called for and I slipped the gold band onto Elaine's finger with surprisingly shaky fingers of my own, to which she returned the favor, and there we were. Officially declared. Husband and wife.

"You may kiss the bride," the vicar said and how I fucking kissed the bride.

I took her face in my hands and I kissed her with all the love in my heart, except it wasn't all the love in my heart. Not anymore. Not now there was the slightest hint of a bump under her wedding dress.

The room cheered, and the exit song sounded out, ready for us to walk back down the aisle as a couple, and that's when Elaine stopped in her tracks, mouth dropping open as she first caught sight of the blonde row of family members, her mother positioned right on the end of a pew.

Her mother, who had tears in her eyes as she clapped for her daughter.

I coaxed Elaine forward but she struggled to look away from her family. There was a whole fresh set of tears in her own eyes as we reached the church porch and the confetti started up around us, a whole new set of cheers sounding out loud.

It was when we were in the back of the wedding limo that she turned to me with those saucer-wide eyes of hers and a billion questions dancing behind them.

"It was you, wasn't it?" she asked me. "You invited my mother here?"

"I did more than that," I told her, and the glee was bursting free as I finally got to tell her exactly what I'd done. I'd sent her mother a recording of the Eddington and Rawlings confession, delivering it straight into her hands through one of my very closest contacts.

I'd sent her undeniable proof that her beautiful little girl has been abused by the sick fucks she'd sent her to spend her weekends with, at the hands of her cunt of an uncle.

I'd sent her undeniable proof that every time

her little girl was sobbing and trying to ask for her help and had been cast aside as nothing but a naughty little liar, she was no damn liar. Not in the slightest.

Clearly it had done its job, since she was here, to watch her daughter marry a Morelli.

Elaine cried. Hard. She cried and thanked me and held me tight, trying to gather the courage to step out to our marquee and see our guests all over again, knowing her mother would be there.

She didn't have to step out very far before Caroline was there to meet her, crying too, giving a declaration that would begin a very long road of forgiveness.

"I'm sorry, Elaine. Please, believe me, I'm so sorry. I never knew...believe me, please, I never knew...I'd have killed that evil bastard myself. I'd have killed them all."

From the very tone in her voice, I believed her.

She held her daughter tight.

Elaine held her right back, sobbing to match, taking a few long minutes before the two of them managed to drag themselves apart enough that I could walk my bride through the manor grounds to our wedding reception and the waiting crowd.

"Let's do this," I said, and she nodded with a

smile.

"Yeah, let's do this, *husband*. I'm ready."

It was time to toast champagne with the hip, hip, hoorays, and give the speeches and cut the cake. We did it. We loved it. We enjoyed every fucking second of it, and then finally, eventually, after the greatest day of my life, I took my wife for her wedding night.

I loved her right through until morning, every little part of her, my wife and my lover.

I loved Mrs. Lucian Morelli-Constantine right through the night until morning, smiling with a whole new smile as I kissed her belly—knowing our little baby was in there.

Thank you for reading the Starcrossed Lovers trilogy! We hope you loved Lucian Morelli and Elaine Constantine's dark and sexy story. Find out what happens next in the Midnight Dynasty world with Lucian's brother, Leo.

The beast hides a dark secret in his past...

Leo Morelli is known as the Beast of Bishop's Landing for his cruelty. He'll get revenge on the Constantine family and make millions of dollars in the process. Even if it means using an old man who dreams up wild inventions.

The beauty will sacrifice everything for her family...

Haley Constantine will do anything to protect her father. Even trade her body for his life. The college student must spend thirty days with the ruthless billionaire. He'll make her earn her freedom in degrading ways, but in the end he needs her to set him free.

The warring Morelli and Constantine families have enough bad blood to fill an ocean, and their brand new stories will be told by your favorite dangerous romance authors. See what books are available now and sign up to get notified about new releases here…

www.dangerouspress.com

About Midnight Dynasty

The warring Morelli and Constantine families have enough bad blood to fill an ocean, and their brand new stories will be told by your favorite dangerous romance authors.

Meet Winston Constantine, the head of the Constantine family. He's used to people bowing to his will. Money can buy anything. And anyone. Including Ash Elliot, his new maid.

But love can have deadly consequences when it comes from a Constantine. At the stroke of midnight, that choice may be lost for both of them.

> "Brilliant storytelling packed with a powerful emotional punch, it's been years since I've been so invested in a book. Erotic romance at its finest!"
>
> – #1 New York Times bestselling author
> Rachel Van Dyken

"Stroke of Midnight is by far the hottest book I've read in a very long time! Winston Constantine is a dirty talking alpha who makes no apologies for going after what he wants."

Ready for more bad boys, more drama, and more heat? The Constantines have a resident fixer. The man they call when they need someone persuaded in a violent fashion. Ronan was danger and beauty, murder and mercy.

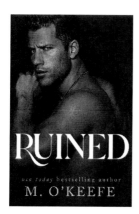

Outside a glittering party, I saw a man in the dark. I didn't know then that he was an assassin. A hit man. A mercenary. Ronan radiated danger and beauty. Mercy and mystery.

I wanted him, but I was already promised to another man. Ronan might be the one who murdered him. But two warring families want my blood. I don't know where to turn.

In a mad world of luxury and secrets, he's the only one I can trust.

"M. O'Keefe brings her A-game in this sexy, complicated romance where you're left questioning if everything you thought was true while dying to get your hands on the next book!"

– New York Times bestselling author
K. Bromberg

"Powerful, sexy, and written like a dream, RUINED is the kind of book you wish you could read forever and ever. Ronan Byrne is my new romance addiction, and I'm already pining for more blue eyes and dirty deeds in the dark."

– USA Today Bestselling Author
Sierra Simone

SIGN UP FOR THE NEWSLETTER
www.dangerouspress.com

JOIN THE FACEBOOK GROUP HERE
www.dangerouspress.com/facebook

FOLLOW US ON INSTAGRAM
www.instagram.com/dangerouspress

About the Author

Jade has increasingly little to say about herself as time goes on, other than the fact she is an author, but she's plenty happy with this. Living in imaginary realities and having a legitimate excuse for it is really all she's ever wanted.

Jade is as dirty as you'd expect from her novels, and talking smut makes her smile.

She lives in the Herefordshire countryside with a couple of hounds and a guy who's able to cope with her inherent weirdness.

She has a red living room, decorated with far more zebra print than most people could bear, and fights a constant battle with her addiction to Coca-Cola.

Find Jade (or stalk her – she loves it) at:
facebook.com/jadewestauthor
twitter.com/jadewestauthor
jadewestauthor.com

Sign up to her newsletter, she won't spam you and you may win some goodies.
www.subscribepage.com/jadewest

COPYRIGHT

This is a work of fiction. Any resemblance to actual persons, living or dead, business establishments, events or locales is entirely coincidental. All rights reserved. Except for use in a review, the reproduction or use of this work in any part is forbidden without the express written permission of the author.

Made in United States
North Haven, CT
25 March 2022

17526675R00169